ISTA

FOR KIDS

CW01658670

Burçak Gürün Muraben
Illustrated by Uğur Altun

CAN ÇOCUK

Editorial Coordinator: İpek Şoran
Proofreading: Sharon Hill
Book Design: Gözde Bitir
Design Application: Recep Eren

First Edition: 2000 copies, June 2014
ISBN 978-975-07-2203-5

© Can Sanat Yayınları Ltd. Şti., 2014
All rights reserved. No part of this book may be reproduced by any process without the written permission of the publisher. Short excerpts may be used for publicity.

Can Sanat Yayınları Yapım, Dağıtım,
Ticaret ve Sanayi Ltd. Şti.
Publisher's Certificate No: 10758
Hayriye Caddesi No. 2, 34430 Galatasaray, İstanbul
Phone: (0212) 252 56 75 – 252 59 89
Fax: 252 72 33 www.cancocuk.com
cancocuk@cancocuk.com

Cover Print: Azra Matbaası;
Certificate No: 27857
Address: Litros Yolu 2. Matbaacılar Sitesi
D Blok Kat: 3 No: 3/2
Topkapı, Zeytinburnu, İstanbul
Internal Printing & Binding:
Türkmenler Matbaacılık;
Certificate No: 12584
Adres: Maltepe Mah. Gümüşsuyu Cad.
No: 16 Zeytinburnu, İstanbul

ISTANBUL FOR KIDS

Contents

FOREWORD AND THANKS

My beloved Istanbul. I was born and bred here. Wonderful friends, lots of chaos, ubiquitous street cats, red tulips, flocks of cormorants and many, many adventures. A husband, two children and another continent later, I am now a Sydneysider.

I wondered how I could pass on my love of Istanbul to my children and their friends. The books I found 'dumbed down' the information or were just infuriatingly wrong. I decided to write a book that had really high quality information, but was quirky and fun, and appealed to both children and adults – an insider's view with and understanding of little outsiders.

I hope it inspires you to find out more, and to come back. I wish you lots of fun and adventure.

Hannah Fink made me feel, the way great friends do, that I can do anything. Big thanks to Banu Akarsu for lots of support and a great collection of books on

Istanbul. Taciser Belge, Jennifer Lianos, Mary Altabev and Nejat Anbarcı made the manuscript better with every comment. I am lucky to have such clever friends. Special thanks to Mine Konakçı for preparing the visuals for my initial pitch.

Selçuk Erez has been encouraging me to do more with myself all my life and introduced me to the wonderful gang at Can Çocuk Yayınları (the publishers). Thank you Samiye Öz and İpek Şoran for making it all plain sailing. I could not have dreamt of having a better illustrator than Uğur Altun. You make me feel truly blessed.

Aslı Özyar, my life-long anchor, helped me see the Museum of Archaeology through her loving and capable eyes. She has had an immeasurable impact on this book.

Thanks also to Frances at Waverly library who said that instead of borrowing books about writing, I should just do it. The staff at Newtown library (the libraries in Sydney are just wonderful) were supportive all the way.

The boring bits are all my fault and believe me they would have been much worse if it were not for Yaz Muraben, Lilah Shapiro and Maya Muraben.

One does need a bit of time away from kids when writing a book and grandmas are made for times like this. Huge thanks to Ida Muraben for that.

And Yusuf, I would have never thought I would say this but 'Thank you for correcting my English' and lightening things up for all of us – no matter what.

THE GALATA TOWER

The Genoese (from Genoa in Italy) built the Galata Tower in 1348. They had ended up in Constantinople after the 4th Crusade in 1204 led by their arch-enemies the Venetians. When the Byzantines re-captured their capital after a 60 year Latin (Roman Catholic) rule, they gave Galata to the Genoese in return for their loyalty and support. By the 1300s, the privileged Genoese were controlling sea trade and flourishing as the Byzantine Empire got steadily weaker.

The 9 storey tower sets you 50m above ground when you are on the observation deck. It used to be surrounded by a moat. The Turkish word for moat is 'hendek'. Have a look around to see if you can find this word in or around the tower.

In 1453, the Genoese presented the keys to their city to the new Sultan – Mehmet the Conqueror. He was only 21 at the time!

The tower was used as a prison for a while. It was conveniently positioned near the dockyards where prisoners could be used as slaves. Eventually it was turned into an observation tower protecting Istanbul from one of its greatest dangers: fire!

I spy with my little eye from the Galata Tower

Still standing proud after 650 years, this medieval tower is where you get a bird's-eye view of the city. Once you figure out the layout of the Golden Horn and the Bosphorus, you get Istanbul. Now climb up the tower and see how many of the following landmarks you can spot:

The Galata Bridge

The current bridge is the 5th to be built on this spot. Nowadays it is covered with fishermen trying out their luck, and it has had a notable history. Michelangelo and Leonardo Da Vinci were both asked to design a bridge. A model of Da Vinci's design, which was rejected, was recently built in Norway. It would have been the longest bridge in the world at the time.

The Golden Horn

This natural harbour used to have a huge chain across it in Byzantine times. You can still see parts of it in the Museum of Archaeology and the Military Museum. In 1453 the Ottomans got their ships across by rolling them on logs over land, straight into the harbour.

Topkapı Palace

This palace was home to Ottoman Sultans for 400 years. It would cover over 1,000 football fields. If you could buy it, it would cost over $10 billion US dollars!

The Maiden's Tower

The Maiden's Tower has been used as a lighthouse and quarantine area. It has also been seen in many movies, including two James Bond films. Nowadays it has a restaurant and café.

The Blue Mosque

The Blue Mosque is the only mosque in the world with six minarets. The reason it got its name was for the beautiful blue tiles inside.

Hagia Sophia

Instead of the tallest building, the challenge in the past used to be the biggest dome. Three famous churches managed to surpass the 30 metre size of the dome of the Hagia Sophia hundreds of years later; any ideas which ones?

St Pauls Cathedral in London, St Peter's Cathedral in Rome and the Duomo in Milan.

The Bosphorus Bridge

Venus Williams played a tennis match on the bridge in 2005, the only match ever to be played between two continents.

Süleymaniye Mosque

The great architect Sinan took on many challenges

including that of Hagia Sophia's dome. Although he didn't make the dome bigger, he managed to make the space underneath the dome bigger in the Süleymaniye Mosque with ingenious design.

HEZARFEN AHMET ÇELEBİ
THE FLYING SCIENTIST

Did you know that you are standing on the actual spot where the ancient dream of flying became reality?

Hezarfen Ahmet Çelebi flew from the top of the Galata Tower and landed in Üsküdar across the Bosphorus using the prevailing winds. This made him not only the first man to fly but also the first man to fly between two continents, from Europe to Asia, and in the 17th century! How cool is that? He studied Leonardo da Vinci's notes on flight of birds and practised flying with wings made of eagle feathers at an archery range.

Evliya Çelebi, the Turkish Marco Polo of the same century talks about the event in his diary. Legend and folklore have given his works a magical quality. He loved travelling and wrote about the customs, buildings and colourful characters he came across.

The Sultan at the time, Murad IV, was in the audience for the flight. He awarded Hezarfen a sack of gold coins and then expelled him! His out-of-the-box thinking was deemed too dangerous. He was sent to Algeria where he died when he was only 31. Very much like Galileo who was sentenced to life imprisonment in 1633 for his brilliant mind. Both politicians and priests found it hard to deal with people centuries ahead of their time.

Initially the Genovese were not allowed to build city walls. Instead they built tall, solid houses next to one another to get around the rule and have some form of defence. The Galata Tower (Tower of Christ) on the northern boundary of the colony was the tallest building in the city when it was completed.

Hezarfen, meaning ‘a thousand sciences’ comes from the Persian ‘hazar’ meaning thousand and the Arabic ‘fann’ meaning science. Persian and Arabic were common languages in the Ottoman Empire.

A favourite subject of Evliya Çelebi was vampire stories. He has written quite a few, and they are some of the earliest vampire stories known!

Little Hagop[1] went to school in Galata in the late 1800s. His teachers had rosy cheeks and domineering moustaches pointing upwards at the ends. He liked spending his lunch breaks on the rooftops daydreaming about "the other side"- the faraway, the remote - Haydarpaşa and Kadıköy were easily visible across the Bosphorous from his perch, just not accessible...

GALATA AND PERA – GATEWAY TO THE OTTOMAN EMPIRE

As the West became more and more powerful following the Industrial Revolution, Pera became the customs port of the Ottomans. Pera is the area separated from the historical peninsula (the Sultanahmet area with Topkapı and the Hagia Sophia) by the Golden Horn. It is now known as Beyoğlu. Many innovations came through here; bridges, the stock exchange, the city council, trams, an underground funicular railway (but with only two stops), modern boat quays, dry cleaners, undertakers, gas and electricity. Galata was the business hub of the city and the main port, but Pera was where you had fun! It was the entertainment centre of the city. The influx of Greeks, Armenians,

[1] Hagop Mintzuri (İstanbul Anıları 1897-1940) was a primary student at the Armenian Getronogan School in Galata. The master of Turkish photography, Ara Güler, is also a graduate of the school.

Jews and foreigners formed the Western character of this part of town early on. There are still many foreign consulates on İstiklal Caddesi, the main pedestrian strip between Taksim and Tünel.

Q and A

Where do you think the name 'Galata' comes from?

a) it comes from the word 'calata' meaning steps in Italian.

b) it comes from the Greek 'galaktos' meaning milk representing the many dairy farms of the area.

c) it relates to the Galatian conquest of the area around 300 BC.

d) it comes from the word 'galeta', a kind of bread-stick eaten by locals.

Answer: Confusing isn't it? Well even experts are still unsure.

FOOD

If you go down İstiklal Caddesi then trying the traditional boiled lollies known as 'Akide' is a must! Ali Muhiddin Hacı Bekir has been making them since 1777. The Janissaries, special forces of the Sultan, were paid four times a year. If everything ran smoothly, the palace distributed these special lollies in celebration of the service and loyalty of the soldiers.

EMİNÖNÜ

THE NEW MOSQUE (YENİCAMİ)

Yeni Valide Camii (the New Mosque of the Queen Mother) is the full name of this mosque built by two Queen Mothers with a long gap in between. It was completed in 1663 so it is not exactly modern but manages to keep young and fresh due to its name, The New Mosque. A Jewish synagogue was demolished and the neighbourhood around it relocated to make room for the mosque. The location was popular with the Queen Mothers due to the fabulous views. Water was pumped out for months to stabilise the ground for the site. One architect working on the site acquired the nickname 'the diver' since he had to go to unbelievable depths to give the seaside mosque a solid foundation.

The New Mosque is a great backdrop for one of the

main pigeon feeding areas of Istanbul. The bird feed sellers are the crankiest, grumpiest and most cantankerous in the city. Legend has it that the Prophet Mohammed was once hiding in a cave from his enemies. A spider made a web and a pigeon built a nest outside his cave which disguised his hiding spot. Pigeons were well taken care of from then on. This is why most mosques have pigeon feeding stations right outside and some have bird houses. From holes in the walls to specially built little homes on the sunny sides of buildings to provide shelter from cats, dogs, rain and snow. You should keep an eye out for these. The one in Yenicami is a little tower. When there weren't bird houses in major buildings, kamikaze pigeons would fly into a window trying to break in. Some died during the mission, others kept trying until they got in. Bird houses kept pigeons alive and the buildings clean.

The Flower Market (Çiçek Pazarı) which has canaries, parrots, monkeys, fish, leeches in jars as well as seeds, plants and gardening equipment is right next door. Buying exotic birds and freeing them used to be a popular pastime in 18th century Istanbul. Monkeys were also really popular and were trained and employed on ships as lookouts!

Don't leave Eminönü without trying the fish and bread from the boats right under the bridge. Turkish bread is to die for; crusty on the outside and soft in the inside. There are plenty of other delicious street food options around. Yum!

The boat trips along the Golden Horn and the Bosphorus all start at Eminönü at different piers. They are definitely worth a try. In the 1960's the pier had a unique attraction: A local seal called Yaşar who used to entertain the crowds from a big boat.

The underground walkway taking you across the street is a whole new world of cheap and cheerful toys and gadgets – basically anything and everything. Keep an eye out for the street vendors in front of the jetties for the latest contraption.

THE SPICE BAZAAR (MISIR ÇARŞISI)

If you love your food, this whole area is a wonderland, trust me. The cheese, the olives, the sweets! All of this is before you enter the Spice Bazaar itself, which takes your senses back a few centuries, particularly by the smell! The Spice Market is loud, fragrant, glittery and quite mysterious. Nuts, powders, lotions and potions, dried roots, leaves, sponges, herbal remedies and spices in huge quantities assault your senses all at once. Take a few deep breaths and take in the smells of the Ottoman palette. Do take your time and hold on tight to your parents. This is a top spot for kids to get lost, like the Covered Bazaar. I am not sure if it is the parents who lose their kids or the kids who lose their parents.

The Spice Market was built to generate money to look after the New Mosque. The Ottoman Empire had to look for new ways to encourage trade and look after merchants after the Silk Route and the Spice Route trade were going downhill after the 16th century.

TAHTAKALE

A walk through Tahtakale is like travelling in time. The wooden toys and the old men still making them in obscure little shops remind me of Geppetto, the toymaker who made Pinocchio. The cobblestone streets twist and turn leading you to one of the main industrial areas of the old city.

Honey, oil, flour and other goods from Russia, The Danube and the Black Sea were all unloaded at jetties along the Golden Horn. Customs control was done in Eminönü. Spices, sugar and cotton from Egypt, India and Yemen were unloaded and stored in the area and sold at the Spice Market.

RÜSTEM PAŞA MOSQUE

The Croatian born Rüstem's sharp mind had come to the attention of Sultan Süleyman the Magnificent early on. He was really good with money too. His mosque, a masterpiece by the architect Sinan, is decorated with the finest İznik tiles. The red carnations and tulips are just stunning!

The Sultan wanted Rüstem to marry his daughter. Jealous courtiers spread the rumour that he had leprosy. The Sultan organised for his stuff to be thoroughly examined and they discovered lice! That was lucky for Rüstem as lice were thought to avoid lepers. Rüstem plotted with the Sultan's wife against Mustafa, the beloved son of the Sultan from another woman and convinced the Sultan to kill his own son! Rüstem eventually lost all his power.

GALATA BRIDGE

The idea of connecting the two sides of the Golden Horn with a bridge had been around for ages. There were many incarnations of this bridge. One of them, the one which burnt down in 1992, was a major part of city life with its fishermen on top and restaurants and coffee houses at the bottom.

The two sides of the Golden Horn were very different from one another. The Galata Bridge brought them closer. The world's oldest (also shortest, it only has two stops!) underground funicular railway between Tünel and Karaköy and the new tramways and piers around Eminönü changed the way the city grew.

The top of the bridge is a great spot to get a view of Istanbul's seven hills. This is how you spot the hills in Istanbul:

- The First Hill has Topkapı Palace and the Hagia Sophia
- The Second Hill has the Nuruosmaniye Mosque
- The Third Hill has Süleymaniye Mosque
- The Fourth Hill has Fatih Mosque
- The Fifth Hill has Sultan Selim Mosque
- The Sixth Hill has Mihrimah Mosque
- The Seventh Hill has three peaks and covers the area around Aksaray.

Why is it called "The Golden Horn"?

Zeus's mistress Io gives birth to a daughter, the nymph Keroessa (which means Golden Horn in Greek), who was the mother of Byzas, founder of Byzantium. The Golden Horn is on the quieter southern end of the Bosphorus and divides the European side of the city into two. It also looks like a golden horn, particularly with the golden light around sunset.

Galata is the only bridge in the world to have a card game named after it. The game is not surprisingly called 'bridge'. The game is thought to be invented by the Russian community of Constantinople. During the Crimean War in the mid-1800s, British soldiers would cross the bridge every day to the coffee houses to play cards.

Like Rome and Athens there are many other cities in the world founded on seven hills. Los Angeles, San Francisco, Tehran, Amman, Melbourne, Barcelona, Bergen, Kiev and Lisbon are a few.

SULTANAHMET

FOUNDATION

It was the fate of Byzas, son of the sea god Poseidon, to found a city which would be named after him. He asked the oracle of Apollo at Delphi for advice. The oracle could predict the future but could not give a straight answer, and Byzas was told to found a city opposite the 'land of the blind'.

Byzas led an expedition to the edge of Europe where the Bosphorus, the channel which joins the Black Sea and the Marmara, joined the harbour called the Golden Horn. Across the Bosphorus on the Asian side was the city of Chalcedon (modern Kadıköy). He thought the settlers must have been blind to settle on the Asian side and ignore the natural advantages and beauty of the Golden Horn. In 667BC he founded an acropolis (fortified city) in present day Sultanahmet.

This area, also known as the Old City became the centre of several empires. The city has since been called Byzantium, Nova Roma, Constantinople and Istanbul as it changed hands. Over the years the Byzantine Empire built the Hippodrome (an enormous horse racing stadium), Hagia Sophia (the mother of all churches at the time), Basilica Cistern (huge water reservoir) and many other amazing features most of which are still standing over a thousand years later.

The Ottoman Empire added a lot including the Topkapı Palace, which was built on the site of the old acropolis, the magnificent Blue Mosque, and the Grand Bazaar.

THE HIPPODROME

The Hippodrome was the heart and soul of Byzantine Constantinople. Hippodrome means 'horse arena' in ancient Greek as does the Turkish name 'At Meydanı'. It was used for many different ceremonies, grand parties, celebrations, circuses and of course the spectacular sporting events. Imagine the deafening roar of 100,000 people all screaming in support of their chariot team. The main teams were the Greens and the Blues (although there were also smaller Red and White teams for a while until they got absorbed by the two major ones). The sport was such a big part of life that supporters followed their teams almost religiously. Like football hooligans they often rioted, and in 532 a particularly big one became known as the

Nika Riots. Shouting and team rivalry became really violent and eventually turned to anger about taxes and the emperor and became a full scale revolution. They set the Hagia Sophia on fire and gathered around the Imperial Palace (which stood where the Blue Mosque is today) trying to break in. After a few days of wondering whether to escape the city, the Emperor Justinian decided to crush the revolt with his army. Over 30,000 people were killed.

Successive emperors erected monuments and statues along the middle of the track. Many have gone, like the 4 enormous bronze statues of horses which were looted by the Latins (as the old Catholic Western Roman Empire of the 13th century was known, long after it split from the Byzantine Eastern Roman Empire) during the 4th Crusade and taken to Venice to become part of St Mark's Basilica. Many monuments still survive – at least parts of them.

When Constantinople became Ottoman in 1453, the Hippodrome continued to be the hub of community life. Many weddings, jareed tournaments (a game played on horseback with a wooden javelin) and circumcision ceremonies took place here. There was a spectacular parade of life size animals made of sugar for Prince Mehmet's circumcision in 1582. You would also find Ottoman acrobats and entertainers hanging from the columns of the Hippodrome.

THE SERPENT COLUMN

Originally over 8 metres tall with a huge golden bowl sitting on three snake heads, all that remains of the Serpent Column today is a bit of coiled green bronze. Around 2,500 years ago the Greeks successfully defended their country against invasion by the mighty Persian army, and created this great monument in thanks to the oracle of Apollo at Delphi. The golden bowl was also stolen by the Latins, at the same time as the 4 bronze horses, and probably melted into coins to fund more crusades. The Ottomans believed the Serpent Column protected the city from snakes and other creepy crawlies. They also believed it was a cure for snake bites. Legend has it that Mehmet the Conqueror cut the heads off when he conquered the city. Once the heads were gone, everyone was sure there were more snakes and creepy crawlies around.

THE OBELISK OF THEODOSIUS

Probably the oldest monument in the Hippodrome is the Obelisk (pointed pillar) of Theodosius. It was originally built by an Egyptian pharaoh nearly 3,500 years ago. 1,800 years later one of the many emperors called Constantine had it brought to the Hippodrome. On the base you can see 'snapshots' from the life of Emperor Theodosius. They didn't have cameras or anything like that at the time so it took quite a while for a sculptor to capture the moment, and you can see some of those moments like a race and victory ceremony.

If you look at the bottom of the base you can see the original level of the Hippodrome 2 metres below the current street level.

THE WALLED OBELISK

This obelisk is thought to be much older than the 10th century, but since Constantine Porphyrogenitus repaired it and put gold and bronze plaques over it, it is named after him. There was a huge sphere on the top, but can you guess who stole it along with the gold and bronze plaques? Those light-fingered Latins!

THE BLUE MOSQUE

You may wonder why it is called the Blue Mosque, when you go inside you will see the beautiful Iznik tiles that give it the name. Normally mosques have one minaret, but if you were a sultan you could have up to four. But even that was considered showing off. Sultan Ahmed I was 14 years old when he became the 14th Ottoman Sultan and ruled for 14 years. He instructed his builders to make him the most magnificent mosque the world had ever seen. And it would have six minarets. This caused quite a stir in the rest of the world.

Only sultans were allowed to enter the mosque on horseback. The gate from the Hippodrome has a chain across the top which would force the sultan on his horse to bow and humble himself before God.

THE COLUMN OF CONSTANTINE

It doesn't look quite as grand as it used to, but when it was originally erected in the middle of the Forum of Constantine it was 50 metres tall and had on top a huge statue of Constantine as Apollo the pagan sun god. He was holding a piece of the 'True Cross' in his hand. Perhaps he was trying to bridge Paganism and Christianity. His mother St Helena recovered many prestigious Christian artefacts from Jerusalem and brought them back to Constantinople. Bronze leaves used to cover the metal hoops that join the sections of the column. Any ideas who might have stolen them?

BASILICA CISTERN

The Roman Empire was great at managing water. Water was very precious and particularly scarce during summer, and storing and distributing it was a huge challenge which they solved with great engineering ingenuity. As the city was often under siege the people

had to have water that would last a long time. So they built several cisterns to store the water, and the largest was under a basilica and so known as the Basilica Cistern (Yerebatan Sarayı or sunken palace) built in the time of the Emperor Justinian. Water would come from 20 kilometres away through the remarkable Roman aqueducts.

It lay unused for a while as the Ottomans preferred running water to still water. A 16th century French visitor to the city saw locals lowering buckets on strings through holes in the floor to catch fish. He followed them and ended up rediscovering the cistern.

The resourceful Justinian harvested many columns from the old pagan temples of his empire for his building frenzy. No one is quite sure why there are two Medusa heads, where they came from and why they are not the right way up, but they are fascinating to look at.

The cistern has over 300 columns, is bigger than a football field and could hold enough water to fill 40 Olympic swimming pools. It has been in movies, video games and is home to countless enthralling art exhibitions including the Istanbul Biennale.

All roads lead to Rome! Rome had a 'golden milestone' which showed distances to all parts of the empire. Not one to be left out, Constantine built his own grander milestone called Million with distances to European cities. You can still see a fragment near the Basilica Cistern.

HAGIA SOPHIA

I was at the age you wonder what God looks like when my grandmother took me to Hagia Sophia for the first time. The light was eerie. The dome which looked further away than the sky took my breath away. It was a scary moment which made me feel very small. I remember thinking that if there were a God, he would surely be here. Suddenly it all made sense. If there were a God, he must be inclusive and here was the proof - a Christian church with big discs on its walls in Islamic calligraphy.

Squeezing the Mother of all churches into shape over the centuries was a hard, thankless job! Have a look at Hagia Sophia from the outside and try to see its support system, the buttresses. Doesn't she look as if she will burst at the seams one day?

The spell of Hagia Sophia has been a 'stairway to heaven' for patriarchs (head Greek Orthodox priests), caliphs (Muslim leaders), emperors, sultans and pilgrims for centuries. The half-domes carry your gaze down from that huge, enchanting and weightless dome like a waterfall. The base of the church is the earth under the dome of heaven. The Islamic script on the dome echoes the older Greek writing 'Peace be with you, I am the light of the world'.

THIRD TIME LUCKY

Hagia Sophia means The Holy Wisdom. The first church with the same name was destroyed by fire during a riot. The second one burnt down during the Nika (victory in Greek) Riots in 532 when both the Blues and Greens, supporters of rival sports teams, united in protest against Justinian's high taxes and tried to overthrow the emperor. Justinian was ready to flee but his wife Theodora put her foot down. General Belisarius turned the Hippodrome into a mass grave for over 30,000 people.

Eager to make his mark on the capital, Justinian started building within a month of the riots, using up

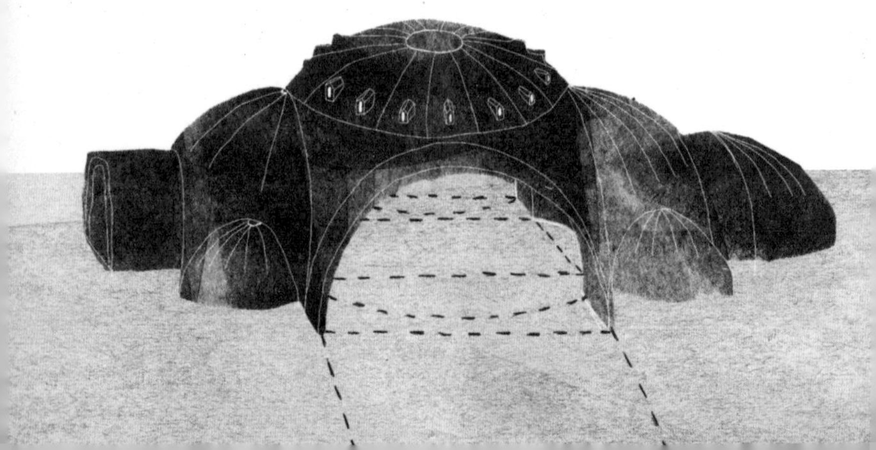

the remnants of the Greek and Roman monuments all over the empire. The new church would be the biggest and the most beautiful in Christendom! The neighbouring Hagia Irene, The Basilica Cistern and the Senate were all completed during this building frenzy.

Two lots of 5,000 workers and 15 master builders worked non-stop for nearly six years, revealing their work on December 27th, 537. Christianity had won over paganism. The dome looked as if it was hanging from heaven, weightless. ‘Oh Solomon,’ exclaimed Justinian ‘I have outdone thee.’ He was referring to King Solomon, the builder of the Great Temple of Jerusalem in Old Testament times.

HOW ON EARTH DID THEY DO IT?

The master builders were Anthemius, a mathematician and physicist from Aydın and Isidorus of Miletus. Isidorus, an expert on Plato and Pythagoras (remember his triangles from school?) had been the director of the brilliant Academy of Athens which was closed down by Justinian because it was pagan (believing in many gods as opposed to one). Both had translated books by Archimedes. The Byzantines translated huge amounts of ancient Greek texts, building a bridge of classical knowledge between the Greeks and the Renaissance.

Anthemius and Isidorus knew their mathematics and started with sketches and calculations before moving to stones and bricks. They tried and failed many times. The huge dome needed special cement, light but really strong. Pozzalana, volcanic ash mixed with lime and water, was already used by Romans and perfect for the job. The building also had to be fire-proof and earthquake-proof. Their bricks were so light they could float. The mortar (cement) was nearly as thick as the bricks. Once it set the bond was very strong. Twenty years later the entire dome came crashing down after an earthquake. Justinian was 76 then and the original architects were dead. Another Isidorus, the architect Isidorus' namesake and nephew, made the dome an oval and reinforced the outside. This was not a rush job, he took his time. A poem about the church said that when the interior was revealed "sorrow fled from the hearts of all, as the sun lit the glories of the temple..."

Hagia Sophia was pretty high maintenance with its staff of 500. They kept their cash register going using it as the main funeral church of Constantinople.

MOSAICS

There were no mosaics in Hagia Sophia in Justinian's time apart from the angels just underneath the dome because Byzantines were unsure whether biblical pictures were OK to show. The mosaics introduced after Justinian's time were destroyed during the 8th century. By the 9th century those in power thought biblical images were OK and were keen to make up for lost time. The Hagia Sophia was Byzantium's favourite documentary channel, presenting the entire history of the Empire from the 6th to 14th century on its walls. Here are some juicy bits from the mosaics:

Emperor Leo VI asking Christ for forgiveness: All poor Leo wanted was a child. No luck with wife number one, two or three. Then his Mistress Zoe Carbonospina (with coal black eyes) bore him a son. Chaos erupted when he wanted to marry her, since the church forbade fourth marriages. He was kicked out of the Hagia Sophia.

Empress Zoe was one of the few women to rule Byzantium. Her father Constantine VIII finally married her off when she was 50 and she went on to have several husbands after the first one. She kept the mosaic master very busy indeed since every time she married, the poor guy had to get the new husband onto the walls quick smart. And making mosaics is much harder than taking a photo...

1204 THE FOURTH CRUSADE: ROMAN CATHOLICS ATTACK BYZANTIUM

The olive branch carried by the dove to Noah's ark after the Flood, Christ's tunic, his stone cradle, his blood and famous crown of thorns were all among Hagia Sophia's treasures. The crusaders, led by the 90 year old Doge (leader) of Venice took them all, including the really heavy altar which ironically caused the ship carrying it to Venice to sink. The idea of Crusaders sacking the centre of Christendom doesn't make much sense does it? The Doge of Venice was blind; if he could have seen the beauty of Constantinople maybe he would not have ordered the plunder. He died soon after and was buried here at the Hagia Sophia at his own request. The Byzantines reclaimed Constantinople in 1261 but the glory days were over. The Hagia Sophia then got a lot of tender love and care from the Ottomans during its next life as a mosque.

1453 HAGIA SOPHIA AND THE FALL OF CONSTANTINOPLE

The last Byzantine Emperors had tried hard to unite the Eastern Orthodox Church with the Western Roman Catholic Church and it eventually happened just before the Turks appeared at the city walls with their cannons. The people of Constantinople were so unhappy they deserted the church. The last Emperor Constantine XI Dragases went to the Hagia Sophia at sunset on Monday May 28th 1453, made his peace with God and re-joined his troops defending the city. The believers prayed all night.

When the Ottoman army entered Constantinople, the soldiers were allowed to loot the city for three days. Mehmet the Conqueror went straight to the heart of the ancient city and humbled himself before God by pouring a fistful of earth over his turban before entering the Hagia Sophia. He became furious with the men trying to steal bits and pieces, scolded them, prayed and turned it into a mosque. His court historian talks about the portrait of Jesus whose eyes, like the Mona Lisa, seem to follow you wherever you are in the church.

Its presence in the heart of the city is a reminder of the city's glorious Byzantine past. The Ottomans did not even change the city's name Kostantiniyye, Arabic for the city of Constantine, which was used for a long time.

FROM CHURCH TO MOSQUE TO MUSEUM

The church was slowly and lovingly transformed into a mosque. Muslim mementos of victory and holy relics replaced Christian ones and crosses. Minarets were added. Royal Ottoman blood allows you one minaret, four is only for Sultans. A crescent replaced the cross on top of the dome and the bells from the bell tower were put away.

A minbar (pulpit) and a mihrab (pointing towards Mecca for prayers) were added. These were at an angle since churches are aligned east-west not like mosques which are usually aligned with Mecca. A medrese (Islamic school) was added.

The mosaics in the lower levels were covered over with plaster since in Islam you can't show living beings as a form of worship. The plaster works ended up protecting them in the long run, so they showed up bright and clear when the time was right to reveal them again!

The Hagia Sophia became a mosque for the funerals of sultans when Selim II was buried there. Two crazy sultans, Mustafa I who spent 14 years in a cage in Topkapı Palace all by himself and lost his mind and Crazy İbrahim who fed pearls and gold coins to the palace fish are buried here as well as the sultans Selim II, Murat III and Mehmet III.

Gazi Mustafa Kemal, the founder of modern Turkey, was given the surname Atatürk (the Father Turk) on November 24th 1934. On the next day visitors to the Hagia Sophia found a note on the gate in Atatürk's handwriting saying that 'The museum is closed for repairs'. He said this important building is best kept as an institute of knowledge rather than a place of worship.

MYTHS AND LEGENDS

There were many myths and legends about the Hagia Sophia, hardly surprising for a building nearly 1,500 years old. The Byzantines loved good stories about the church to help blend it into everyday city life and the Ottomans were great storytellers, so they made sure there were enough myths, legends and stories connecting the Hagia Sophia to the Muslim population. Here are a few:

Justinian drops holy bread during mass and a speedy buzzing bee grabs it and flies away. All beekeepers are ordered to search through their hives for the bread. A hefty reward is promised. A beekeeper turns up with a very intricate and weird looking hive.

This becomes the design of the Hagia Sophia.

All workers are out at their lunch break and the architect's son is minding the tools inside the church. An angel appears and asks him to fetch everyone so they can finish the job faster. He promises to mind the tools until the young boy returns. The young boy tells his father what happened and his father cleverly refuses to send everyone back in, thinking that the angel will protect the church forever. The angel was said to be seen ascending to the sky a few days before the fall of Constantinople, leaving the church and the city without protection.

The winged angels just underneath the dome were believed to be talismans (to ward off evil). Even before the birth of the prophet Mohammed they alerted the city of Istanbul to danger.

The 'Christian' dome collapsed on the day of the Prophet Mohammed's birth and could only be repaired with special mortar made from holy sand and water from Mecca held together with a dash of the Prophet's saliva.

The doors are said to be made of wood from Noah's ark.

The 'sweating column' was said to help women wanting babies and people with eye problems over the centuries. Now, put a finger into the hole and twist it. If your finger comes out wet, your wish will be granted, if dry, bad luck.

‘Manarah’, an Arabic word meaning lamp, lighthouse is related to ‘manar’ candlestick, which comes from ‘nar’ fire. The Hebrew word ‘menorah’ meaning candlestick is from the same root too. The Muslim minarets and the menorah, the candle holder, an ancient symbol of Judaism are closer to one another than you think!

Ho! Ho! Ho!

St. Nicholas was a Byzantine priest who secretly put coins in stockings that were left out by the poor and needy. The secret gift giving eventually made him popular as Father Christmas.

In the early 1990’s, I had an English friend visiting Istanbul. She had a look around Sultanahmet and came back raving about the pink of the Hagia Sophia blending in so beautifully with the clouds. ‘What do you mean’ I said, ‘the Hagia Sophia is yellow – ochre – call it what you want but it is definitely not pink’. ‘I was just there’ she said ‘it is pink.’ ‘I have spent twenty years looking at it’ I said. ‘It is yellow’. She won the argument. They had just painted it!

TOPKAPI PALACE

Mehmet II conquered Istanbul in 1453 at the tender age of 21 and started building his imperial capital. He wanted to do better than the Roman Empire and impress the Europeans. He was both eastern and western in his ways and wanted to rule the world. He started a building frenzy with new neighbourhoods blossoming around mosques. Schools, public kitchens and baths (hamams) followed. Buildings providing charity were supported by money-making shops. Rent from shops at the Covered Bazaar made sure the Hagia Sophia was always well looked after. Whole communities of Jews, Muslims, Greeks and Armenians were lured to Constantinople with promises of opportunity and wealth. Anyone was welcome as long as they kept out of trouble and paid their taxes. Trade boomed in the safe and trendy capital. The new royal court thrived with Persian poets, Arab and Greek astronomers, Italian scholars and artists.

Topkapı, the palace of the Conqueror, was completed in 1465. The name Topkapı means 'cannon gate' and took its name from a nearby gate in the city walls opposite which the Conqueror placed his cannons. Why here? Well spotting invaders is easy, it's isolated and safe from rebellion and plague and looks across from Europe to Asia. It has a great view too...

The remains of Byzantine buildings were used to finish the job quickly. Many empires recycled parts of buildings from previous civilisations.

When the Ottoman army went to war they camped in tents. Topkapı has the same design as the military camp sites but in bricks and mortar. The sultans believed in humility before God and didn't want to show off by building flashy palaces. The palace grew 'organically'; new buildings would replace old buildings which perished in fires or started to fall apart with age.

THE IMPERIAL GATE

Mehmet the Conqueror wrote a message on the gate. 'Enter then, in peace and security'. This courtyard was protected by 50 Royal Guards. Anyone could walk into it as long as they didn't have weapons or umbrellas (which could conceal weapons).

! GORE ALERT The Ottomans displayed the heads of traitors on hooks on the walls as a warning much like the English did at London Bridge.

THE FIRST COURTYARD

The little church on the left is Hagia Irene (Holy Peace). It was never turned into a mosque because it was within the palace boundaries. It is now a popular concert hall with its magnificent acoustics.

25,000 Janissaries attended the funeral of Mehmet II in this largest of the palace courtyards. The Ottoman army band 'Mehter' performs here at 3pm on Wednesdays. The Ottomans loved using music to inspire their soldiers and to frighten their enemies. A hospital treated the royal pages (the Sultan's attendants) with music and herbs. Some pages faked illnesses so they could visit their families since they hardly ever got to leave the palace.

Closer to the Middle Gate were workshops for carpenters, miniature artists, stonecutters, tailors and weavers where Turks, Hungarians, Albanians, Armenians, Persians (modern day Iranians) and others worked together to make the best wares in the Empire. Some of their most exquisite works are on display at the Topkapı Museum. The palace employed a total of 360 artists in the year 1500 and nearly 1000 in 1600.

! GORE ALERT The Executioner's Fountain is where the executioner washed his hands and sword after executing prisoners. Executioners could not be buried in public cemeteries – they had a special cemetery with no writing on their modest tombstones.

GATE OF SALUTATION

People had to dismount their horses here as only

the Sultan could ride beyond this point. This was the VIP gate for the court. Complete silence was a tradition enforced by attendants with white wands. Imagine ten thousand people gathering here for a banquet and eating in utter silence! After the 16th century, a sign language called Ixarette was introduced and mutes were employed as teachers. Deaf mutes were hired for secret assassinations as it was easy for them to keep secrets.

The Sultan kept 30 of his favourite horses close in the Royal Stables for hunting or riding in the surrounding woods. The stables also had camels and mules. A bit further up you can find the luxurious carriages used by the sultans and their families.

! GORE ALERT Just beside the gate, there are two marble blocks where the heads of high ranked offenders were displayed. One in six viziers (ministers) had violent deaths.

THE TOPKAPI KITCHEN

The Palace kitchens fed the poor as well as palace folk and visitors. The Sultans loved showing their generosity with elaborate trays of feasts.

Food, desserts, medicines, soap and endless preserves were prepared here. Some oil caught fire while frying kebabs in 1574. The wind carried sparks to the Harem and started a fire. The great architect Sinan made the chimneys taller for safety.

Kuşhane was the Sultan's private kitchen and his water was brought daily from a spring above the

Golden Horn guarded 24/7 by the Janissaries. The Sultan and Queen Mother preferred to eat from bowls made from special ceramics called celadon because they were believed to change colour when poisoned. The service was very orderly and efficient. 200 waiters formed two lines between the kitchen and the sultan's quarters. One row passed along the food and the next passed back the empty dishes. White bread was quite a luxury. Only the Sultan and the Queen Mother had white bread, and the Grand Vizier and his family if they were in the good books, everyone else ate the dark coarse bread.

Up to 6,000 meals were prepared here every day. 1,000 staff brought the kitchen to life during the busy holy month of Ramadan. The menus were legendary and the portions were generous. 60,000 sheep, 200,000 fowl, 25 tons of honey and a ton of salt were consumed every year.

The palace had about 600 confectioners in the 16th century who wore tall white hats that looked like cake decorations. They went in and out of the palace as they pleased and did pretty well for themselves by doubling the price of everything they bought from outside for the other inhabitants who were not allowed to leave the palace grounds.

Breakfast was bread, fruit and jam served at 10am. Boiled mutton, stewed vegetables, rice, sherbets (sweet cordials from which we get the word sorbet) and molasses were served for lunch at 3pm. The Ottomans started their meals with dessert and ate

their way to their greens! Meals were served in simple bowls, usually with wooden spoons. Water was drunk from golden cups chained to basins. No lost cups and minimal washing up!

THE IMPERIAL COUNCIL

This is where the big bosses met. The Grand Vizier (Prime Minister) would lead the meeting while the Sultan watched behind a secret window with a golden grill. The curtains were always drawn so nobody could see if he was there or not. The Valide Sultan (the Queen Mother) had peeking rights. When the Sultan tapped the grill or drew the curtain it was time for the viziers to present their reports one by one.

TOWER OF JUSTICE

15 storeys high, it represents the just and watchful eye of the Sultan on the city. It is inspired by the portable wooden tower the Ottomans used on military campaigns. Anybody could come to seek an audience with the Sultan. Justice was really for all.

THE GATE OF FELICITY

This is the gate to the sultan's main residence 'a light, happy palace open to the fresh air and pure sunshine of heaven.' Everyone needed the Sultan's permission to enter. Consider yourself lucky walking through this gate because the only foreigners who were allowed here were ambassadors, and only by special appointment. Smiling was banned in the presence of the sultan since to be dignified a face had to be stern!

The gate was guarded by the white eunuchs, teachers at the palace school Enderun. This is where the coronation of new sultans took place. The Sultan would also mingle with his subjects and officials here during important religious holidays twice a year.

Janissaries would get their wages four times a year. It was a very festive but orderly occasion. The Sultan would make a haughty appearance. 5,000 Janissaries would bow to the passing commanders in complete silence.

This meant trouble. If they were unhappy about something they would show their disapproval by refusing to eat their soup.

Q and A

How did the palace know if the Janissaries were unhappy about something?

a) They sent a messenger to the Grand Vizier
b) Their band Mehter played a special tune
c) They wouldn't drink their soup

Answer: (c)

The palace loved showing off to the foreign ambassadors so they were regularly invited when the Janissaries collected their salaries to see the spectacle. The Sultan would receive ambassadors in the Audience Chamber. Two porters led the ambassador by the arms to the middle of the room and made sure his forehead touched the ground as he bowed. The Sultan kept his haughty silence during the presentation. The visitors had to leave quietly, shuffling backwards. Gifts were exchanged and then came coffee, sweets, sherbet, perfumes and a meal.

CHAMBER OF PETITIONS

This is where the Grand Vizier and council members would report to the Sultan. They could be showered with gifts, receive a promotion or end up strangled by the deaf mute eunuchs depending on their performance. Never a dull moment!

THE PALACE ACADEMY

The palace academy Enderun was founded to create well educated and sophisticated palace staff and Janissaries. The graduates of this very strict boarding school ruled the empire for centuries. The Ottomans recruited bright and handsome Christian boys, mostly aged from 8 to 10, from farming families in the Balkans. This system was a huge success for 250 years producing loyal and qualified people for the empire.

The boys marched all the way from their villages to Istanbul. When they completed their training they swore loyalty to the Sultan and their fellow soldiers on a tray containing salt, the Koran and a sword. The symbols of their regiments were tattooed on their legs or shoulders.

The brightest were selected for the academy to be educated as pages. One of the tests was seating everyone around a long wooden table with soup bowls in the middle. Everyone was given ultra-long wooden spoons and asked to finish the soup as fast as they could. The brightest ones figured on that the quickest way would be to cooperate – they would feed the boy opposite as they were fed by him.

All boys were converted to Islam. They had to stand on the threshold of the Gate of Felicity for three whole days during their initiation before being led into their dormitories which would be their homes for years to come. Classes started at 5am. They were taught languages, mathematics, astronomy, history, religion, music, swordsmanship, riding, wrestling, javelin and philosophy. Food, manners, hygiene, sleep... everything was done by the rules. They graduated after ten years. They would kiss the Sultan's sash, receive their ceremonial kaftan, jewels, a fine turban and money and were considered part of the Sultan's wider family. 400 pages lived in the palace, half studied while the other half served the sultan. The best pages joined the '39 elite of the Sultan', the Sultan himself making 40, a number special to the Ottomans.

The sultans were protected around the clock. Mehmet II had four pages watching him in pairs while he slept. They were trained to keep their eyes on him without making any movement. The silahdar watched the arms and weapons, the çuhadar looked after his clothes, the rikabdar looked after the footwear and a

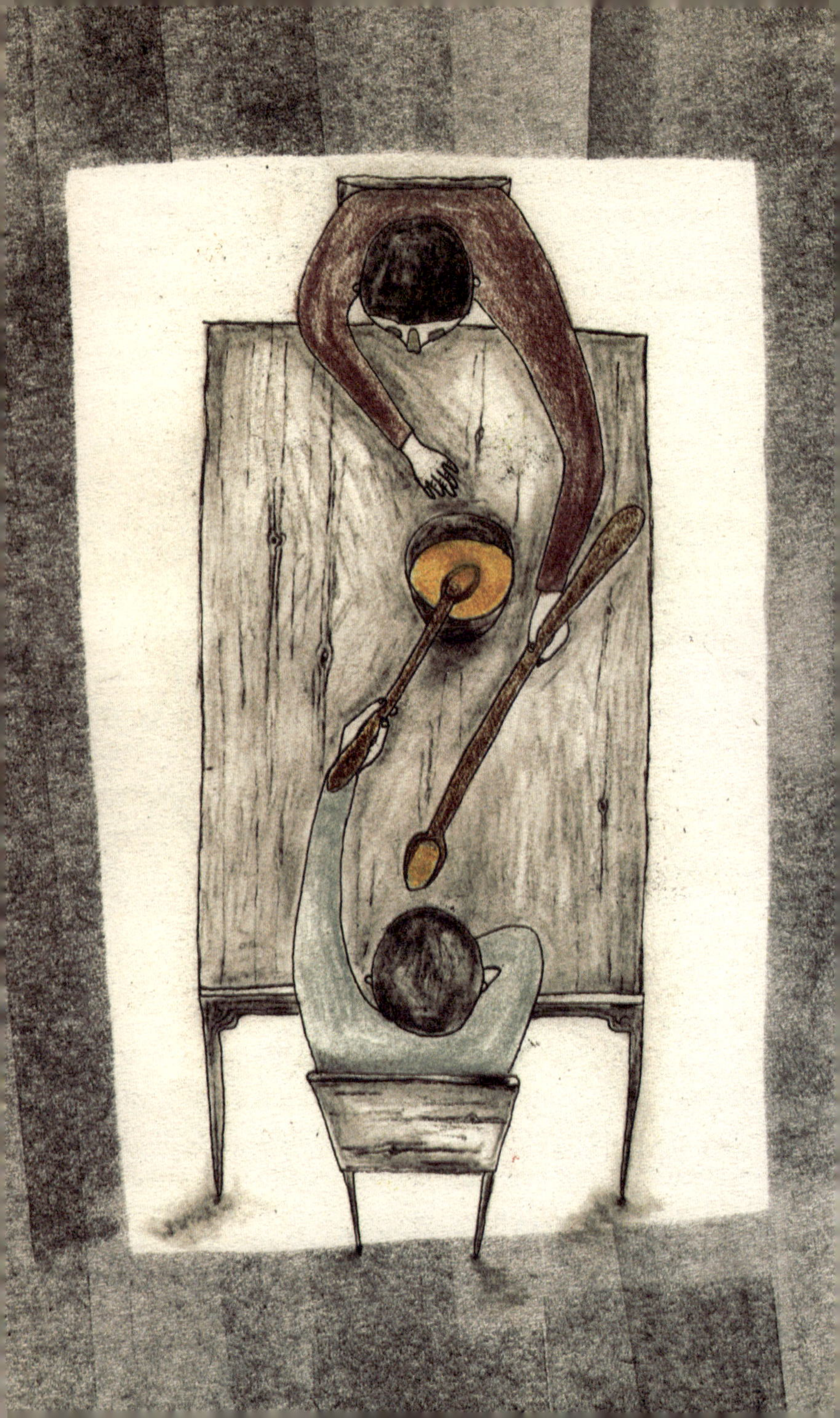

fourth page was allocated to take care of the Sultan's turban. Washing the metres and metres of muslin cloth which made up the Sultan's turban was an important job. Pages would be responsible for the Sultan's manicure and pedicure, laundry and serve as masseurs and bath attendants on campaign.

THE HAREM

The word Harem comes from the Arabic for sacred or forbidden. The Ottomans, like the Byzantines, kept palace women and children isolated. The women only moved to the Harem at the Topkapı Palace in the 16th century. Christian girls who were technically slaves converted to Islam, learned Turkish, music, literature and needlework at this 'palace prison'. They made educated wives for the Ottoman elite and produced heirs to the throne.

The Valide Sultan (the Queen Mother) ruled the harem. The wives of the Sultan, the concubines, their children and their servants all lived here. The Chief Black Eunuch was the administrative boss of the Harem.

Graduates of the harem had a few options. They could hit the jackpot by marrying the Sultan and becoming Queen Mother one day. Most married a graduate from the academy and started a family. To celebrate the recovery of the sultan from an illness or the circumcision of a prince, some would be freed to marry outside of the palace.

EXHIBITS FROM THE MUSEUM

The dormitory of the royal pages houses the 'Portraits of the Sultans' exhibit.

Q and A

What facial feature was prominent in the Ottoman dynasty? Not hard to work out is it?

Answer: The Nose

IMPERIAL TREASURY

This is where you will find the famous emerald studded dagger. Sent as a gift to the Shah of Persia, it arrived after the Shah's death and therefore was taken back. I guess it was not meant to leave the palace after all.

Various amazingly ornate thrones are displayed here. There is the enormous 86 carat 'spoon maker's diamond'. Found by a poor man and exchanged for three wooden spoons or so the legend goes. The spoon maker sold it to a jeweller for 10 cents and it eventually made its way to the palace. Check out the tiny thrones and cradles for the sultans' children.

CHAMBER OF THE SACRED RELICS

The most sacred relics of the Muslim world are kept here. The Koran is read non-stop. These relics confirmed the Sultan the legitimate leader of the

Islamic world and protected the Ottomans against evil, just like the Christian relics that protected the Byzantines. The cloak of the Prophet Mohammed, one of his teeth, a hair from his beard, two swords and a bow, the swords of the first four Caliphs, the staff of Moses and the turban of Joseph are all here. It was so sacred that even the Sultan and his family were only allowed here only once a year.

THE FOURTH COURTYARD

This is a series of gardens with pavilions like the Baghdat and Revan kiosks. The palace doctors lived here. The Master Magician's main job was to prepare a calendar predicting when to go to war or to start building a new mosque.

Elephants, giraffes, lions, tigers, bears, wild boar, gazelles, deer and goats lived in the grounds of Topkapı. The wild boar were hunted by the Sultan and named after his enemies like the Duke of Florence and the Grand Master of Malta. Peacocks and ostriches wandered freely. The original eggs were brought from Mecca as a souvenir of pilgrimage (Haj).

The number 40 represents 'many' for the Ottomans where we might say 'hundreds' and it is a special number in Ottoman culture.

- Mohammed became a prophet at the age of 40.
- It took 40 years for Adam (as in Adam and Eve) to be created.
- In times of great danger, Muslims would pray for 40 hours.
- The Turkish for centipede is kırkayak (forty feet).
- Once in a blue moon is once in every forty years.
- Ali Baba had 40 thieves.
- 40 copper coins equalled a kuruş.

When Sultan Murat the 4th heard Evliya Çelebi recite the Koran at the Hagia Sophia he was mesmerised and invited him to live at the palace. The sultan was quite a large man who liked a bit of a wrestle. One day he holds Evliya by his hands and starts spinning him in the air. Evliya, terrified, tells the sultan that he needs to fart badly and gets him to put him down.

The Ottomans concealed voices with the background sound of running water whenever they needed privacy. If a room had a fountain, it was likely to be a meeting place where you could have secret conversations.

GRAND BAZAAR

My favourite entrance to the Bazaar is through the Nuruosmaniye Mosque Gate, the first big Baroque mosque in Istanbul. I often get lost (this is the most fun way to have a look around, but do stick close to your parents) but the shopkeepers and locals are always helpful with directions. I love wandering around finding new places. The light filtering through the trees onto ancient buildings gives the whole place a really magical feel.

I like to walk down Yağlıkçılar Street in the Bazaar and see material being sold as it has been for hundreds of years. If by chance you end up by a barber shop, and you are lucky enough to see them showing their amazing shaving skills, wait until the end and you will be amazed how they remove hairs from the ears – with fire!

After leaving the Bazaar I like to walk downhill through Mahmutpaşa to Eminönü. Everything is much cheaper here as the shopkeepers don't pay the massive rent they have in the bazaar. You'll see shops selling all sorts of things. Some sell capes and sparkly hats, and you might even see little boys parading around in these rather elaborate circumcision outfits. This is a ritual celebration for Muslim boys. They have a big party with lots of presents as this represents their coming of age.

THE HISTORY

When empires changed in 1453, Constantinople was desperate for a major makeover to become the buzzing capital Mehmet the Conqueror had in mind. New neighbourhoods started with a mosque – the centre of daily life for Muslims. Charity, one of the five pillars of Islam, is very important so imarets (where travellers and the poor were looked after) and medreses (religious schools) were built nearby. Looking after these and the mosque required money so local craftsmen produced goods and merchants sold them at the bedestan – a special covered market. The bedestan gave a city status since it meant international trade, wealthy people and a big population. It had offices for merchants and stored precious goods as well as jewellery and money owned by ordinary folk, like a bank. Cevahir (jewellery in Arabic) Bedesteni – now home to furs, kaftans, carpets, antique guns and harnesses – was the first bedestan of the Covered Bazaar. People did anything they could to get a shop here. It was even harder to become a night watchman. Who do you think chose them? The mighty Sultan himself!

The second market, Sandal Bedesteni was built to

support the Hagia Sophia. The neighbouring streets full of shops eventually joined in for safety and convenience. They all got under cover and formed the mall which was called 'the Covered Bazaar' from the 18th century onwards. The whole bazaar was locked up meticulously every night and a visit after dark required a note from the Sultan. It was once used as a party venue to celebrate the return of Sultan Abdülaziz from Egypt. He arrived on horseback and had all the streets to himself. James Bond, on the other hand, preferred the rooftops of the bazaar for an awesome motorbike chase in the movie 'Skyfall'.

Thieves used to dream about the place. 30,000 gold coins were stolen in 1591. Life came to a complete stop for two weeks until the money was found hidden under floor mats and the culprit was executed.

EVLİYA ÇELEBİ

Auctions for slaves were held here too. Sultan Ahmet bought a slave girl and her brother in the slave market in the Covered Bazaar. The girl was given to an old soldier and they had a son called Evliya. When he grew up Evliya became a famous writer and opened a very vivid window into the 17th century Ottoman Empire with his observations, legends and stories. The other boy from the slave market was his uncle and went on to become the Grand Vizier (Prime Minister) and son-in-law of the Sultan. Rags-to-riches stories like this were, unlike in Europe, common among Ottoman nobility.

What do you make of the bird sculpture at the main

gate? The Evliya said poetically "Profit is like a bird. If you can catch it gracefully, you will succeed".

THE PEOPLE

Greeks, Turks, Armenians and Jews worked and played together drinking infinite glasses of tea and coffee and wearing colourful shoes. Turks used to wear yellow shoes, Greeks blue, Jews black and Armenians red. Some of the craftsmen and merchants were women. The Italian writer Edmondo de Amicis talks about the haughty tones of the Greek merchant, the cunning but humble Armenian, the Jew whispering to his customer about the discount he is getting, and the pa-

tient Turk sitting quietly in front of his shop. He would overhear greetings in many languages 'Monseigneur, caballero, captain, signor, excellency.' Nowadays you can't tell a seller's background from their shoes. They are really out there and in-your-face. Young teenagers switch easily between languages and cultures like old hands. Where do they all come from? That's a tricky one. All over the place is the answer – wherever the buyer is from. If the buyers speak Spanish, so do they. Arabic with a French accent? not a problem. French with a dash of German... well you get the idea.

Once they tune in to your language, the fun part starts - haggling.

HAGGLING

In Istanbul, like many other cities, you can haggle a little in stores, but the haggling that goes on in the Grand Bazaar is out of this world. When you want to buy something in the Grand Bazaar it is rare to pay the price the shopkeeper originally asks. Here are some rules for haggling.

Always be polite. Shopkeepers are trying to make money after all, and will try to sell their wares for as much as they can but they will never be rude. When haggling start by offering half the marked price.

If more than one shop sells the same item and you want to find the very lowest price, you must offer a price that is too low and leave the store. That's right, leave without buying anything at all. It is common for the seller to say no to your offer and if you turn to leave all of a sudden they will accept it. So you never know if they might go any lower unless they actually say no and you go to the next shop and offer a little more.

If you want something specific don't come right out and say it. When a shop knows you really want something you will have a hard time getting the price down, but if you pretend you want 'something similar, but I guess that might do' they will be more willing to drop their prices to convince you to buy. When you do buy something it is common to be offered a cup of tea and share some stories.

GUILDS

Every craft group like velvet weavers, cushion dealers, cap makers and booksellers had its own street, corridor and little courtyard. When traders of the same goods reached a certain number they had their own club called a guild. Once the guild was formed, it controlled the rules, prices and taxes.

When an apprentice learned the trade, he presented his works to the guild members hoping to be accepted with a special belt and some good advice. 'Be patient, be clean, do not steal, do not covet someone else's property, remember the graces you receive, forget the evils'. His works would then be sold on a silver tray and he would open his own shop with the earnings. When a guild member died, his son replaced him. If his son wasn't interested or unable to take over, the business was sold.

There was a `procession of the guilds` before the Sultan. They prepared shows and had clowns and wild animals for entertainment. The great hullabaloo ended with a lavish feast at the Sultan's table. They included some pretty weird guilds including beggars, lunatic asylums, bear trainers, liver and tripe merchants, water carriers, soothsayers and makers of lady's slippers.

Goods of extraordinary value were traded, but honesty and fairness were valued above all! In the beginning, shopkeepers supported each other rather than competing, prices were fixed and haggling was bad form. There were no security guards during the daytime, people would leave their shops unattended for ages (in the beginning they didn't even have windows). As the empire declined the quality fell and corruption took over. Making money became harder and shopkeepers started competing for clients and haggling became the new way.

Süleyman the Magnificent learnt how to make jewellery from a Constantine in Trabzon when he was a prince. His teacher Constantine got really angry with him one day and said that Süleyman deserved 1,000 strokes of the cane. His mother was devastated and asked him for forgiveness. Constantine would not budge. So Süleyman made 500 very thin wires out of fine gold strands. He was caned with these twice on his feet to make the 1,000 lashes.

THE MUSEUM OF ARCHAEOLOGY

Have a run around Gülhane Park and go into the Museum of Archaeology to catch your breath. You might find the million or so objects here overwhelming. Many civilizations thrived in Turkey and the Ottoman Empire ruled over archaeological treasure chests like Syria, Iraq, Palestine and Egypt. Some of the finds eventually dispersed all over the world. Some were looted and smuggled; a few were given away as presents.

In the 18th and 19th centuries Western Europeans collected ancient Greek and Roman sculpture and artwork in their museums to show they were as powerful as their mighty ancestors. They could also afford to look after them, which always helped. Art and archaeology went hand in hand. Osman Hamdi Bey, who studied Fine Arts in Paris, founded the first Fine Arts Academy and Museum of Archaeology under one roof. Drawing and collecting ancient and beautiful objects was a fundamental part of education.

FINDERS KEEPERS?

Ottomans founded their own museums to display the rich cultural heritage of the empire. Treasure hunting Indiana Jones style was a big no-no in the Ottoman Empire; you needed an excavation permit by the Sultan himself. 'Digs' were often sponsored by European countries and the finds were split between the Ottomans and the excavators. People loved telling stories with objects. What you collected and how you displayed it showed what you valued, and hence who you were.

MUSEUM OF THE ANCIENT ORIENT

A pair of lions made by the descendants of the mighty Hittites protects the entrance of this small but exciting museum. What do you think they are made of? Basalt, a kind of volcanic rock! Now head over to the

hall of reliefs from the Citadel of Zincirli and look for a man and a woman sitting at a table with food between them. Any luck? The food looks like flat bread or 'pide', the Turkish word for pizza. You should try some!

THE HISTORY OF WRITING

Here the story of writing comes to life.

Q and A

Where do you think were the first writers from?

a) Mesopotamia
b) China
c) Egypt
d) Central America
e) All of the above

Answer: Probably all of the above but Mesopotamians (modern day Iraq) have the oldest evidence. Clay tablets from around 3,000 years ago have been found in Mesopotamia with records of how much wheat or how many animals people had. Proper writing as we know it probably appeared around a few hundred years later.

Writing turned out to be much more useful for controlling people than armies. The pen really is mightier than the sword. Imagine having ten thousand people under your rule thousands of years ago. Well, it makes sense to write things down to keep track of food, taxes, laws and trade.

What do you write on and how do you keep it? Clay is everywhere and easy to shape but without baking it perished quickly. Sun baked clay survives for ages. The British Museum re-bakes Mesopotamian tablets to preserve the information on them.

Writing first started with pictures of objects called pictograms. If you wanted to write birdbath you would draw a bird and a bath. How about the word belief? Early writers solved this problem by dividing words into syllables they could draw. Bee + leaf = belief. When you read it out loud, you hear belief. This is when writing became phonetic. Phonetic roughly means pronounced as it is written. Turkish, by the way, is one of the most phonetic languages in the world. It would have been fun creating all those signs for a new language. Have you seen the movie Avatar? James Cameron got a team of linguists to create a new language for the movie. J.R.R. Tolkien who wrote 'Lord of the Rings' and 'The Hobbit' was a master of languages and created several languages for his fictional universe. Does "Minionese" ring a bell? What movie is that from? Despicable Me

Assyrian merchants brought writing to Anatolia. Hittite, the earliest Indo-European language known to have been written down, is the grandmother of Latin and Greek which in turn were parent languages for English, French German any many others. Proverbs, cures for poison, the oldest love poem in the world (which is put on a special pedestal on Valentine's Day), multiplication tables and samples of school work in cuneiform can all be found in the museum.

The Hittites and their languages: the more the merrier!

Hittites used many languages including the languages of their neighbours and of the people they conquered. They had two writing systems. Luwian hieroglyphs, like Egyptian ones, were made up of either pictures of the words they represented or syllables.

Using the Hieroglyphic Luwian key below, can you find the symbol for 'king'?

You could mix and match the pictures and syllables which make our writing look very boring!

The ancient scribes used bamboo sticks to write on clay. Europeans studying this writing in modern times noticed that the signs looked like little wedges and called it cuneiform, which comes from the word for 'wedge shaped' in Latin. Like Chinese, cuneiform had some signs for syllables, some for sounds.

TREATY OF KADESH

The Hittites and Egyptians fought for what are now Syria, Lebanon, Palestine and Israel for over 200 years. Both sides lost many soldiers at the famous Battle of Kadesh but there was no clear winner. The treaty, a promise of eternal peace, was actually signed 15 years after the battle of Kadesh and does not even mention it!

It is one of the oldest surviving written treaties. We know the exact wording. Both the Egyptian and the Hittite versions have survived, which is fantastic because we can compare them. It was signed by

Luwian hieroglyphic in pictures

Hieroglyphic Luwian in syllables

A cuneiform alphabet

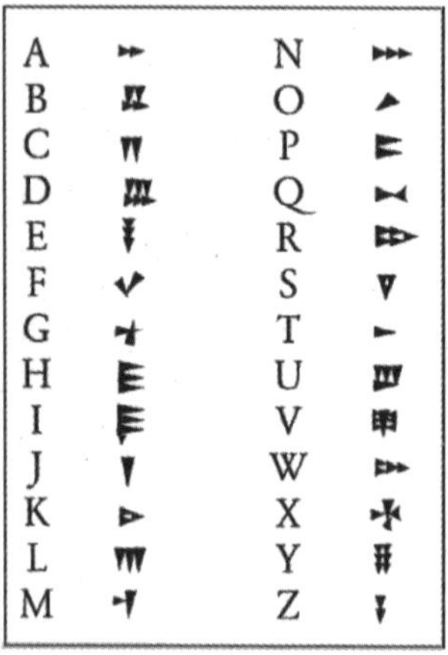

How would you write your name in cuneiform?

Ramesses II on the Egyptian side and the Hittite King Hattusili III. A third and very significant signatory was Queen Puduhepa. Not many women signed peace treaties in those days. Puduhepa was a great diplomat and dedicated to peace, but the peace in her own house was destroyed when she decided to have her daughter marry Ramesses II. The bride, who didn't have a say in the deal, was not happy at all!

Two of the three tablets of the treaty are here at The Museum of the Ancient Orient. The third is at the Berlin State Museum. The Headquarters of the United Nations in New York City also has a copy on permanent display.

THE TILED PAVILION

This beautiful pavilion was built in 1472 by Mehmet the Conqueror to watch the Ottoman 'derby games' between the Cabbages and Okras. The Ottomans used the same colours as the rival chariot teams of the Byzantines: the Greens (Cabbages) and the Blues (Okras). The first games started at the beginning of the 15th century between the towns of Amasya, famous for its okra and Merzifon, known for its cabbages. Both teams were about 200 strong. The Cabbage Obelisk at Topkapı is erected to commemorate Selim III's shooting of an egg at 408 paces at the games. Needless to say, he was a Cabbage! The Okra Obelisk commemorates a similarly impressive shot by Mahmud II in 1811.

These derby games, organised for a bit of fun and battle practice among the students of the palace academy, often got so out of hand that the sultan himself had to intervene to stop them. 'Tomak', played between two teams of six, was played with a leather ball filled with felt attached to a whip. The players had to be very speedy and agile to escape blows by their opponents. Once you were hit, you were out. The last one standing won. There was also handball, played with balls made of wood. Once the ball was thrown, the players tried to catch it mid-air. Enderun, the palace school, offered excellent equestrian training. The best riders would be so skilled they could shoot an orange on the head of their opponent while both parties were riding at full speed. The best horsemen were given special horses by the sultan.

The Tiled Pavilion is now part of the Museum of Archaeology and has wonderful exhibitions showcasing the traditions of famous ceramic centres like Selçuk, İznik, Kütahya and Çanakkale.

ANCIENT SCULPTURE IN ANATOLIA

There is a fantastic range of mythical and historical ancient Greeks who had the western Turkish Coast as their homeland. You can find Zeus, Hera, Athena, Sappho, Hermes, Apollo, Poseidon, Dionysus and Pan to name a few.

Why do you think statues of Athena show her wearing Medusa's head?

Perseus was the son of Zeus and Danae, a mortal woman. The oracle at Delphi told Danae's father that he would be killed by his grandson, Perseus. Sent out to sea, mother and son washed up on an island, whose king wanted to marry Danae but saw Perseus as an obstacle. He threw a party where he asked everyone for gifts. He asked Perseus for Medusa's head.

Medusa, the mortal one of the Gorgon sisters used to be a very beautiful girl. She was cursed and ended up having snakes for hair and eyes that would petrify (literally turn into stone) anyone who looked into them.

Perseus prayed for help from the gods and received a helmet of invisibility from Hades, winged sandals from Hermes and a shiny shield from Athena. Perseus crept up on Medusa without looking directly at her eyes, but her reflection in his shield, and cut off her head with one quick blow of his sword.

On the way he stopped by Ethiopia where he rescued Andromeda who was about to be sacrificed to a monster and took her as his bride.

When he returned home he showed Medusa's head to the king which immediately turned him into stone. He presented it to Athena who always wore it from then on. After their deaths Athena set Perseus and Andromeda as constellations in the sky which we can still see today.

ALEXANDER THE GREAT'S SARCOPHAGUS (WHICH ACTUALLY DIDN'T BELONG TO ALEXANDER)

It is the summer of 1887. A farmer in Saida (now Lebanon) discovers a big old tomb as he is digging a well. Osman Hamdi Bey, the director of the museum, rushes over to supervise the excavation which reveals a city of the dead! 26 sarcophagi (ornate coffins)! The sarcophagi are so large and heavy that transport is a problem. Legend has it that Osman Hamdi Bey, worried about its safety, ties himself to Alexander's Sarcophagus as it is being winched onto the boat. When the German Emperor Wilhelm II visits Istanbul he asks the Sultan for the sarcophagus. Osman Hamdi Bey says 'over my dead body!'

The main building of the museum was built for this collection and it resembles one coffin in particular: 'The Weeping Women'. The Pergamon Museum in Berlin was specially built to house and exhibit the famous altar from Bergama in Turkey together with other finds from the site.

Now, let's see if you can find Alexander. He claimed to be a descendant of Hercules, who killed the famous Nemean lion as the first of his 12 labours and wore the skin as a trophy. He is the one with the lion's pelt wrapped around his head! He is fighting the Persians in one long face and hunting in the other. He was the leader of the Greeks (Macedonians to be more specific) fighting the Persians (modern day Iranians). How can you tell the two sides apart? Can you spot any differences in their clothes? The Greeks are wearing short tunics and the Persians are in long sleeved shirts with many layers. Persians were not allowed to show flesh, but showing a bit of face and the tips of the fingers was OK. Originally the hair, eyes, lips and clothing were painted in vivid violet, yellow, blue, red and purple with the flesh areas given a slight varnish. Check out the coloured example in the hall to see how it would have looked.

Now, have a good look at the clothes of the people in the hunting scene. Can you still tell them apart? Do you think they are still enemies? Well, no. After he captured Persia, Alexander wanted to bring the Greek and Eastern worlds together by behaving and dressing Persian himself, all the way. Clothing, tradition, even his wife – everything was Persian. Here Greeks and Persians are hunting together.

OTHER COOL EXHIBITS

The 'Istanbul through the ages' exhibit on the 1st floor will give you an idea of the adventures of the city. Check out the massive chain the Byzantines used to lock off the Golden Horn. Talk about chunky – each link was 25 kilograms! How did the Turks get past then? The chapter on the Walls of Theodosius has the details.

'Anatolia and Troia through the ages' on the 2nd floor has artefacts from the legendary Troy. The Odyssey and Iliad, poems of Homer, are all about the famous war which Helen of Troy started with her legendary beauty – 'the face that launched a thousand ships'.

Queen Puduhepa lived with her husband the Hittite Great King Hattusili III in a huge palace on top of a citadel protected by high towers and mighty walls. She was pen pals with the Egyptian Pharaoh and his wife and even had her own seal to use on letters and treaties.

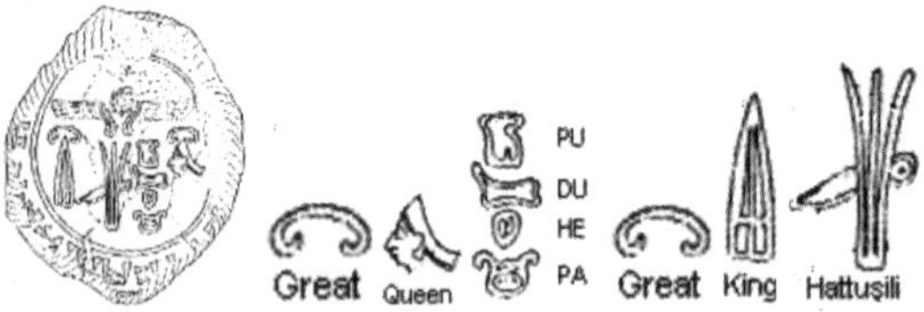

Try making your own for your next birthday invitation, making stamps from potatoes is easy.

Every Turkish kid gets into kuşdili (bird's language) at some stage. It is similar to 'Pig Latin'. You add an extra syllable beginning with the letter 'g' and ending with the vowel in the previous syllable. Ottoman would be Ogottogomagan.

Learning was a special treat in ancient Mesopotamia. Kids went to 'tablet houses' to be taught and disciplined by 'big brothers'. I hope there weren't any bullies around! They had to make their own clay tablets then learn to make marks in the soft clay.

Do you know when English, French and German were first written? About 2,000 years after the first Hittite tablets! The clay tablets in the museum are among the earliest examples of Indo-European writing.

The purple coffins in front of the main entrance are made of the purple marble porphyry. Purple was the royal colour of the Roman and Byzantine empires.

SÜLEYMANİYE

SİNAN THE ARCHITECT

As the Ottoman Empire expanded into new territories it became very wealthy and turned some of this wealth towards very ambitious building projects. There weren't many architects around and when the Chief Architect died the Grand Vizier (Prime Minister) of Süleyman the Magnificent gave the job to Sinan.

Probably Greek or Armenian in origin, Sinan of Karaman was recruited as a 'devşirme'. These were strong and clever young boys recruited from the Balkans by the Ottomans. They were converted to Islam and trained at the Palace School. Some became Janissaries (special soldiers of the Sultan), some personal servants to the Sultan, some even went on to become Grand Vizier. The downside was that they had very little contact with their own families.

Trained as a carpenter, Sinan accompanied Sultan Süleyman on four military campaigns where he built impressively large siege engines, long and sturdy bridges and always finished on time. He studied buildings and renovated old mosques between battles. He became chief architect in 1538 and graced the city with over 300 wonderful buildings for 50 years.

All his life he dreamt of the perfect dome over a huge space. It was the great design challenge for over 1,000 years. He found creative and elegant solutions to the problems. His designs are reminiscent of St Peter's Basilica in the Vatican and St Paul's cathedral

in London. Süleymaniye is his most glamorous work in Istanbul, but his real masterpiece was the Selimiye Mosque in Edirne.

SÜLEYMANİYE

Süleyman the Magnificent, known to Turks as 'The Lawgiver', loved his wife Roxelana 'The Joyous' dearly and gave her a mosque designed by Sinan on her birthday in 1538.

Although the darling wife of the Sultan, Roxelana was not popular with the people. They called her 'The Witch' for talking the Sultan into having his own son (from a different mother) murdered. Her plan worked out and their son 'Selim the Sot' (he drank a lot) succeeded Süleyman but it all went downhill for the Ottomans from there.

The Sultan was heartbroken when his eldest son Mehmet died of smallpox when he was 21 and commissioned Sinan to build the Şehzade Mosque in his memory.

Süleyman was 54 now, a mature and successful monarch on the throne for 30 years! He asked his Chief Architect for something unique, simple and majestic – the Süleymaniye – a wonderful centre of learning. It included the imperial mosque, a primary school, a medical college, religious schools (medreses), a hospital, an insane asylum where they used music as a form of therapy, a public kitchen that catered for teachers, students and the poor, a market, a public bath. It had two tombs – one for Süleyman and one for his beloved wife Roxelana. Süleyman's tomb has his trademark huge white turban on top. The Ottomans were world leaders in astronomy because of the complicated calculations of prayer times and calendars using the sun, moon and stars and Süleymaniye had a very famous astronomy school.

Süleymaniye was completed in 7 years and became the most important Ottoman monument in Istanbul. Legend has it that Süleyman the Magnificent grew rather impatient towards the end. He arrived at the mosque unannounced to see Sinan calmly smoking a water pipe right in the middle of the floor.

Q and A

What do you think he was doing?

a) Sinan had bronchitis and needed the water pipe to help him breathe

b) He has been testing the acoustics of the hall

c) He was reflecting on how to punish a carpenter who was caught stealing

Answers: (b)

Sinan had learnt a lot from his restoration of the Hagia Sophia and although the dome of Süleymaniye was not quite as big, the design was far more ingenious and the sense of space inside with its simplicity and enormous undivided room was truly grand. Sinan had also worked out the air currents through the windows so masterfully that all the smoke from the many candles gathered in one particular area. He condensed the smoke in a special room to make a very high quality ink which was used in the calligraphy on the walls.

The interior space of a mosque important because of the way men pray together. Muslims answer the call to prayer from minarets 5 times a day. You will become familiar with this sound during your stay in Istanbul. Most important are the Friday prayers where men stand side by side facing Mecca and follow the leading imam in prayer. On special days the mosque can fill up quickly and the need for open space is easy to see.

Süleyman was the 4th sultan to rule from Istanbul, hence the 4 minarets. The 10 balconies on the minarets (called şerefes) indicate that he was the 10th sultan after Osman, the founder of the Ottoman Empire.

Süleyman the Magnificent was an early animal rights activist. He issued many decrees to protect the animals which carried construction materials for the Süleymaniye. He made sure the animals were well looked after and never overloaded.

THE WALLS OF THEODOSIUS

The sea took care of Istanbul's defences, north, south and east. Men walled off the west. Within these walls was 'the city'. Until the end of the 19th century Istanbul was still a walled city. It was taken only twice in 1,000 years. Once by the Latins (Roman Catholics) during the Fourth Crusade of 1204 and once by the Ottomans in 1453. These grand walls still remind us of the men and women who built them to embrace their beloved city.

Now back to the year 328. Constantinople was the capital of Byzantium, the new Roman centre of Christendom. Its people spoke Greek but the government was run in Latin. The growing population needed more space and better protection. They reclaimed land from the sea and built walls around their city.

Getting regular food and drink were major problems for medieval cities especially in times of siege.

The Roman network of aqueducts brought water 400 kilometres to underground cisterns in the city.

Theodosius II came into power in 408 with a protector to help him as he was only 7! The Goths had captured Rome and the Huns were threatening Constantinople. The dedicated, hardworking protector Anthemius gave New Rome (another name for

Constantinople) new walls on seven hills (coincidentally old Rome also had seven hills). Everyone chipped in – even the Greens, Blues, Reds and Whites, eternal rivals at the Hippodrome. They joined forces competing for who would work better and faster. Greens went north from the Sea of Marmara and the Blues started from the Golden Horn. The 7 kilometre inner walls were completed in 413 when Theodosius turned 12. They were 5 metres thick and 12 metres high – the size of a 5 storey building.

The earthquakes of 447 hit the walls hard. Attila the Hun was breathing down their necks, but all the king's horses and all the king's men somehow managed to put the walls together again. And in just three months! The city's defences were better and stronger than ever before.

You would be welcomed by a moat which was flooded under threat. Then came a low wall followed by the outer walls with nearly 100 towers alternating with the inner walls. The area in between now has gardens and orchards. The inner walls had their own high towers. These new walls not only scared off Attila, but protected Constantinople for 1,000 years until the invention of gunpowder and its devastating use by the Turks.

Do not try this at home!

Great balls of Greek fire! These sticky balls of flame kept on burning even in water. They were a nightmare for enemy boats. The recipe was the best kept secret in the Empire. It was probably a form of petrol thickened with resin so it would last longer on water. They set fire to attacking Ottoman siege weapons and to the soldiers climbing up the city walls.

YEDİKULE AND THE GOLDEN GATE

Four Byzantine and three Ottoman towers form the Castle of the Seven Towers (Yedikule), which is now a museum. The Ottomans used two of these as a prison for foreign ambassadors who got into the bad books of the Sultans. There is graffiti in many languages on the walls of the Tower of the Ambassadors. Sultan Osman was executed here at the age of 17 by Janissaries (the Sultan's Special Forces) who were not happy with his reforms.

! GORE ALERT The heads of executed prisoners were displayed at the "example stone" at the Topkapı Palace and their bodies were sent out to sea through the hole in the ground.

The Golden Gate was a V.I.P. Gate reserved for Emperors. The last ride in triumph through the gate by an emperor was during the recapture of Constantinople from the Latins (Roman Catholics) in 1261. The gate was later walled for good after many defeats.

BELGRAT KAPISI (BELGRADE GATE)

Süleyman the Magnificent brought many artisans back from Belgrade when he conquered the city in

1521. They settled here and named the area around the largest Military Gate. Turks are the only nation still building city walls in the 20th century owing to the restoration projects of the 1980's.

SİLİVRİ KAPI (PEGE GATE)

Greek troops entered the city through here in 1261 to reclaim the city.

If you have time the Church with Fish, Pege (Balıklı Kilise), is a Byzantine church dedicated to the Virgin Mary which is worth the detour. The outer courtyard has tombstones inscribed in the Karamanlı script (Turkish written in the Greek alphabet). Down the steps from the entrance of the church is a holy spring. The legend goes that one day a youngster called Leon came across an old blind man who was very thirsty. A ghostly voice told Leon where there was a spring. They found the spring and the old man splashed some water on his eyes and suddenly he could see! The same voice told Leon that he would one day be Emperor and when this came true he built this church.

On May 29th 1453, the day Constantinople fell, a priest was frying fish when a messenger gave him the bad news. He said he could only believe when the fish in his frying pan jumped into the spring (something like when pigs will fly), and that was exactly what they did! From then on the fish in the spring became brown on one side and red on the other, or so the story goes.

Just outside this gate, is the grave of Elekli Dede

(Sheikh with Sieves) who only ate sieves! Yes metal sieves used to sift flour! He would throw the wooden bits away like eggshells and devour the rest. He was mute and apparently a nudist, rather fond of the Gypsies of the area whom he often followed around.

MEVLEVİHANE KAPISI (GATE OF THE REDS)

The Reds repaired this gate after the great earthquake of 447 and got the naming rights to it. Mevlevihane Kapısı (Mevlanakapı) is named after the whirling dervishes who stood outside the gate.

TOPKAPI (THE CANNON GATE)

Within the walls between the Sea of Marmara and the Golden Horn Constantinople changed emperors in the year 1453. The Lycus Valley (Bayrampaşa) allowed the walls between the gates of Topkapı and Edirnekapı to be vulnerable as the defenders were stuck well below the attackers. The river was where Vatan Caddesi is now. Sulukule, the playground of the Gypsies since Byzantine times, was here just inside the walls. It was recently demolished.

THE SIEGE OF CONSTANTINOPLE

By 1453 Byzantium was poor and worn-out by civil wars. The Ottomans threatened from East and West, by land and by sea, making their way to the last bastion of the Byzantines – Constantinople. The Byzantine Emperor did all he could to prolong the inevitable. He paid Ottomans taxes, agreed to 'military assistance' and even gave his son Manuel to the Ottomans as a hostage for security.

Mehmet gathered materials from older buildings and made his Grand Viziers compete with each other and managed to get Rumelihisarı completed in just 4 months. Together with the fort called Anadoluhisarı on the other side of the Bosphorus built by his grandfather (Bayezid I), he gained full control of traffic along the Bosphorus. All passing ships had to stop and pay a toll, those who didn't pay got executed.

Byzantine emperors and the Roman Catholic Church had a big fight over how much man and how much God Jesus was. The patriarch (head priest) of Constantinople despised the Roman Catholics and said 'Better the sultan's turban than the Pope's mitre' after the Latin (Roman Catholic) invasion of 1204-1261. The emperor, desperate for help to defend the capital, finally united the two churches, but the people deserted the Hagia Sophia in disapproval. On April 1st churches around the empire celebrated Easter while the Hagia Sophia stood dark and silent. Five days later the Turks arrived. By the end of April the Ottomans had lost 35,000 men and the Byzantines 5,700. Mehmet II gave the Byzantine Emperor one last chance to surrender. The Byzantines said they would rather die defending their beloved city.

Cannons, invented in the 15th century, revolutionised siege warfare. The Romanos Gate was called Topkapı (The Cannon Gate) since the Conqueror placed his biggest cannon opposite the gate. The Hungarian cannon master Urban started off with the Byzantines but changed sides when he wasn't paid. He promised his cannon could turn even walls of Babylon to dust. Mehmet II was quick to spot the potential and offered him four times what Urban was asking from the Byzantines. Three months later the bronze monster 'The Imperial' which fired 600 kilogram stone balls was ready. The next challenge was taking this monster to the city walls. The Gate of Romanos and the Palace of the Blachernae were the two weakest links in the walls. Teams of Ottoman carpenters and engineers levelled hills and built bridges. 60 oxen had to pull the cannon more than 200 kilometres from the foundry to the walls of Constantinople at a rate of 4 kilometres per day. It could only be fired seven times a day because it overheated badly and took ages to cool down. The Ottomans fired at the tired city walls, punching out the corners of squares in the walls. When the centre was hit the whole area would collapse.

The Byzantines were thrilled at the arrival of Venetian Giovanni Giustiniani Longo with two ships and 700 men. He was put in charge of the Romanos Gate. A clever and courageous soldier, Longo discovered that loose rubble absorbed the cannonballs much better than solid bricks. Every afternoon, cannon fire would turn a large portion to rubble. Every evening the people of Constantinople would patch the walls with wooden stakes and anything they could find. You can see some of these huge balls just inside the gate.

The Fifth Military Gate was named as Hücum Kapısı (The Gate of the Assault) after 1453. When Giovanni Giustiniani Longo was wounded and had to be carried away to a ship, people thought he was fleeing and lost heart.

Tuesday the 29th of May 1453 was the day of the final assault. It was pure mayhem with smoking cannons and Byzantine fireballs. The Ottomans created as much noise as they could with tambourines, cymbals, trumpets and terrifying war cries. The Janissary band (Mehter) was egging on the Ottomans and terrifying the Byzantines who were trying to counter by ringing all the church bells in the city at once. Byzantium fell. Mehmet II was now 'Mehmet the Conqueror'. Tuesday is still considered an unlucky day for Greeks.

The city was plundered for three days. The loot they stole was how the soldiers got paid in those days. On the fourth day the Byzantines became Ottomans. Mehmet the Conqueror saw himself as the new Roman Emperor. He wanted to reunite Rome and Constantinople and rule a new Muslim world empire. He appointed the Greek Orthodox patriarch in 1454 and his successor still leads the Greek Orthodox faith today from the Church of New Rome in Istanbul.

The Virgin Mary had been the greatest protector of Constantinople. The city had many holy relics to help. The Byzantines saw her image on the walls which inspired them to beat the earlier siege of 1422 by the Ottomans. Even the

Ottoman attackers swore they saw a woman in purple robes walking along the top of the walls.

The Byzantine Emperor Constantine Dragases agreed to give the Ottomans land 'as big as a cow's hide' when Sultan Mehmet asked for land for a hunting lodge on the Bosphorus. The clever sultan cut the cow's hide into really thin strips joined at the ends and encircled the huge area where Rumelihisarı, the Throat Cutter tower, stands today. Viewed from above the tower resembles the word 'Mohammed' in Arabic script.

EDİRNEKAPI (THE GATE OF THE CEMETERY)

The Chora Museum, like the Hagia Sophia, started life as a church and was retired as a museum after spending much time as a mosque. The decorations, mosaics and frescoes we owe to Theodore Metochites, an all-rounder: a diplomat, theologian, philosopher, historian, astronomer, poet and patron of the arts.

He got into the bad books of the next emperor and after a few years of banishment came home. Chora was looted during the Fourth Crusade in 1204. During the siege of 1453 since it was so close to the city walls the Byzantines brought images of the Virgin Mary here to help protect the city.

The mosaics show scenes from the life of Jesus and the Virgin Mary which were very popular in the middle ages. 'The First Seven Steps of the Virgin' shows her when she was only six months old! The Virgin and Joseph is another interesting scene.

There is a story about when the Virgin Mary was ready to get married. Priests accepted bids from local suitors. Each suitor placed their staff on the altar and the priests prayed for a sign. Joseph's staff began sprouting leaves so he got to marry her. The family album starts with the Virgin Mary's pregnancy and ends with Jesus visiting Jerusalem for Passover.

GATE OF THE WOODEN CIRCUS

This gate was left open and unguarded for a few moments in May 1453. The Janissaries grabbed the opportunity and waved the Ottoman flag over Constantinople for the first time.

TEKFUR SARAYI - THE PALACE OF THE ONE BORN IN PURPLE

Purple was the royal colour of the Byzantines (like the Romans). Being born in the purple meant you were born son of the Emperor in the special purple room in this impressive palace which was built in the 13th century. After the conquest it was home to elephants and giraffes and other large but well behaved animals. A visitor complained about a giraffe kissing him on the neck in the 16th century. Famous for its pottery in the 18th century, it was a refuge for the poor of the Jewish community during the first half of the 19th century.

EĞRİKAPI - THE CROOKED GATE

On Mon 28th 1453 the spirit of the city changed. Everyone gathered at the Hagia Sophia, the spiritual heart of Byzantium. For a brief moment Christianity was united. Constantine in his final speech said the Byzantines, sons and daughters of Ancient Greeks and Romans, were a great and noble people. He thanked the Italians for their help, prayed and left for his palace. He said goodbye to everyone there, asking for forgiveness for any wrongs he had done. Not a single eye was dry. He rode to Eğrikapı to have a last look at the Ottoman troops preparing to attack and rode off to his command post ready to die for his beloved city.

Constantine, son of Helena, was the first Eastern Roman Emperor. The longest chain of unbroken monarchy ended over 1,100 years later when another Constantine, son of another Helena, perished here at Eğrikapı with sword in hand defending his beloved city and faith. Greeks believe he will come back when the time is right and erected a statue of him in Athens.

THE PALACE OF THE BLACHERNAE

The best way to go is through Dervişzade sokak. The first palace here was built in the 6th century near a very sacred spring. It was then turned into an extravagant palace. The Latin (Roman Catholic) Emperors used to live here and took all its riches back to Italy. Blachernae was the mother of all sacred springs in Byzantine Constantinople. The church built over it used to house the mantle and robe of the Virgin Mary. Constantinople was her city and the churches dedicated to her outnumbered all others. The Prisons of Anemas are a part of the palace where unpopular emperors ended up.

The walls always needed men to defend them. An army was costly and could turn against the Emperor, so the emperor only had a small group of foreigners as bodyguards. The Scandinavian Varangian Guard, the 'axe bearing barbarians', came as pirates first, then traders and then ended up as the trusted guards of the Emperors. They fought particularly bravely against the Roman Catholics of the 4th Crusade. The only trace of them left in the city is a carving of the name 'Halvdan' in Viking runes in the Hagia Sophia.

THE SEA WALLS ALONG THE GOLDEN HORN AND MARMARA WALLS

You can have a good look at the sea walls on your way to and from the airport if you take the coastal road (sahil yolu). These walls were eventually extended to meet the land walls and seal the city defences. A steep hill called Petrion was where the Byzantines built a fortress. In 1204 the Fourth Crusaders talked the Byzantines into lowering the chain blocking the

Golden Horn (you can check it out at the Museum of Archaeology on the second floor) and got into the harbour. Entering the city through the sea walls was a piece of cake! The Ottomans amazed everyone in 1453 by rolling their 72 ships on greased logs over the hills of Pera into the Imperial Harbour. Mehmet the Conqueror was so impressed with the defenders of Petrion that he awarded this brave lot with many privileges after the battle even though they fought against him.

ST SERGIUS AND BACCHUS

Called 'The Little Hagia Sophia' by the Turks this church was completed in 527 during Justinian's building frenzy. The previous emperor who had thought Justinian was plotting against him pardoned Justinian after a dream in which St Sergius and St Bacchus told him there was no plot. Justinian built this church with a sigh of relief! There used to be fire-fighting equipment kept here, now taken to the Fire-fighters Museum (İtfaiye Müzesi). The coffeehouses around the church were popular hangouts for fire-fighters.

How Yenikapı got its name: the Ottoman Sultan Murat the 4th liked dressing up as ordinary folk and mingling in. One day he took a boat from Üsküdar and asked the other passenger what he did for a living. He said he was a fortune teller. Murat asked him if he knew where the Sultan was. The fortune teller replied that he was on sea. 'Near or far?' asked the Sultan. 'Well he is with us! And since I am Ahmet the Fortune teller, you must be the Sultan.' was the reply. The amused Sultan had another question. 'If your answer is correct, I will give you the world, but if not you will regret it. Through which gate shall I enter Istanbul?' The fortune teller wrote his answer on a piece of paper and presented it to the Sultan and asked him to read it once he was inside the city walls. The Sultan went ashore and approached the walls and asked the guards to create a brand new gate for him. He read the fortune teller's message after entering through the newly opened gate. It read 'Your Majesty, may your new gate bring you luck and fortune!' From then on, both the gate and the area were called Yenikapı, the New Gate.

THE BOSPHORUS

The magic, the beauty and the foundation of the city of Istanbul is the Bosphorus which both unites and separates two seas and two continents. Can you put the continents Europe and Asia on the map? Hint the word 'Asia' literally means 'the land of sunrise'.

It is hard to believe that the beautiful Bosphorus is full of traps with its sharp bends and sinister currents. The surface currents go from the Black Sea to the Marmara whereas the deeper ones go the opposite way. Around 8,000 years ago the Mediterranean rose after a huge earthquake and spilt its excess waters into the Black Sea. This is how the Bosphorus was born.

Before the bridges were built, all travel was by boat and you felt the power of the Bosphorus every time you crossed between continents. Swimmers had to know their currents and swim accordingly. The bridges let you hop back and forth between Europe and Asia as many times as you like. The views are great too but the real fun is on the boats with the spray of salty water on your face or a sudden encounter with a huge ship the size of a floating continent. Dolphins and the seagulls love playing hide and seek with the boats and steamers.

Q and A

How did the Bosphorus get its name?

Zeus and Hera are husband and wife. Zeus turns his mistress Io into a heifer to hide her from his wife's rage. Any ideas what a heifer is?

a) a chestnut coloured horse

b) a cow who has not yet had calves

c) a type of butterfly

Answers: a cow who has not yet had calves

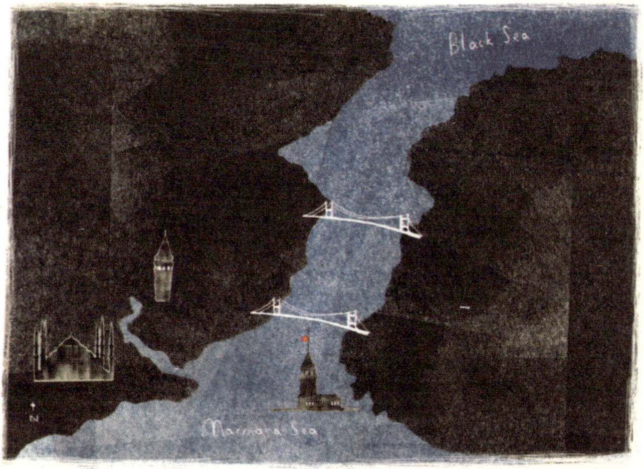

Q and A

The furious Hera sends a relentless horsefly to pester Io who swims from Europe to Asia to escape and gets to name the Bosphorus (which means 'cow crossing')! There is a very famous university town in England whose name also means crossing of cattle. Any ideas what it might be?

Answers: Oxford.

Q and A

Jason and the Argonauts after the Golden Fleece

Then there is the legend of Jason on his way to the Black Sea to Colchis (present day Georgia) looking for the Golden Fleece. The goddess Athena had given the ship Argo (whose name meant "swift") a special power. What was it?

a) It could talk

b) It stayed afloat no matter what

c) It could become invisible

Answers: It had the power of speech and could tell the future

Legend goes that until their arrival, there were clashing rocks which crushed any ship crossing the Bosphorus. Jason and the Argonauts managed to immobilize these rocks and secured Greek access to the Black Sea.

CROSSING THE BOSPHORUS

In 490BC The Persian Emperor Darius lined up his ships and walked his army across them. I guess you could call this the first bridge.

The Bosphorus froze in 1011 and 1232 turning it into the world's most spectacular ice-skating rink. In January 1621, it snowed for fifteen days straight in Istanbul and the frozen Bosphorus was where everyone wanted to be – but on foot.

In 1844 an Italian visitor to the city who took off from Üsküdar in his red balloon was swept into the Marmara Sea by a strong wind. He eventually managed to control his balloon around the Princes' Islands but freaked out when he realised that a seal was racing

him below. As he went higher, the winds swept his balloon farther away. It took the poor man hours to land.

The first bridge on the Bosphorus was between Ortaköy and Beylerbeyi. It was completed in 1973 on the 50th anniversary of the Turkish Republic. The second one, between Rumelihisarı and Anadoluhisarı, opened in 1988. Can you mark them on the map? The second bridge is the spot where the Persian King Darius took his army across from Asia to Europe about 2,500 years earlier. The bridges are normally for vehicles only but you can walk on the first bridge when it is closed to traffic for the Eurasia Marathon every October.

ORHAN PAMUK'S BOSPHORUS

Orhan Pamuk, who got the Nobel Prize for Literature in 2006, loves books and said that Istanbul is 'a place where readers from all corners of the world can live another life, just as credible as their own.'

In 1990, Orhan Pamuk's Black Book changed the city's perception of its waters. He painted a fascinatingly putrid picture of the Bosphorus drying up and turning into a swamp with ship wrecks, green sewers and poisonous gases, rats running amok as the whole area is quarantined as a desperate measure to control lethal epidemics. This was a very serious warning that the Bosphorus needs more care. The sewage system of a huge city on an international seaway with crashing oil tankers is a disaster waiting to happen.

THE INDEPENDENTA

The Bosphorus is a very busy body of water with nearly 50,000 ships travelling through it every year. Every now and then huge ships either collide with one another or smash into the living rooms of the poshest residences on its shores.

When I was in high school I was revising for an exam in our living room which had views of the Bosphorus. Well after midnight I closed my eyes to go over the details of the siege of Constantinople. Seconds later I opened them into another world. A red one! A loud explosion and more red followed. It was Independenta – a Rumanian oil tanker which exploded after a collision with another tanker in 1979. People died, the Bosphorus was black for a month. 30,000 tons of oil burned, 60,000 tons became part of the Bosphorus. 96% of sea life perished.

THE MAIDEN'S TOWER - KIZKULESİ

This tiny island off Üsküdar had inspired many legends. Hera and Leander were lovers. Their families didn't approve, so the lovers met secretly. Hera lit up Leander's path with a torch leading him to her tower every night. On a very stormy light, the light was on, so Leander started his trip but drowned after the light went off. Hera in despair took her own life. It appears that the legend actually belonged to the Dardanelles further south.

There is a Turkish legend about a nobleman locking up his daughter in the Maiden's Tower for protection. A fortune-teller had told the family that the girl would be bitten by a serpent in her teens and lose her life. The prophecy was fulfilled when a snake found its way to the tower hidden in a basket of grapes.

The Maiden's Tower was used as a lighthouse, quarantine area during the cholera epidemic of 1830 and a customs control point. It participated in the city's defences in 1453. Now it houses a restaurant and café.

In 1990 a group of poets devastated and furious to discover that such a historic and beautiful building was being used to store rat poison declared the Maiden's Tower to be a Republic of Poetry and founded a symbolic poetry library in the building.

CRUISING THE BOSPHORUS

This is a must! If you have two days in Istanbul, spend one day on a boat and you'll love it. The boats usually start at Eminönü. The old part of town,

the Topkapı Palace, the Hagia Sophia and the Blue Mosque all look stunning from the sea.

DOLMABAHÇE

The palace was built on reclaimed land (hence the name which means 'filled-in garden') in mid-19th cen-

tury when the Ottoman sultans wanted a more modern, European looking palace. The only way to visit this elaborate baroque palace is by taking part in a tour.

Atatürk, the founder of modern Turkey died here at 9.05 am on the 10th of November in 1938. All the clocks in the palace are frozen at this time. Every year the whole country commemorates the death of its first leader at this time.

ORTAKÖY

Ortaköy is a vibrant little village which has a beautiful Baroque Mosque, a synagogue and a church merely metres from one another. 'Köy' means village in Turkish and there were many along the Bosphorus with their own places of worship, fishermen and local produce. Ortaköy is right before the European support of the first bridge and has handicraft markets among its wooden houses and its cobblestone streets on the weekends. Under the Asian support is Beylerbeyi Palace and Kuleli (the one with the twin turrets) the Military College.

BEBEK

Bebek is very pretty. Right next door to the Egyptian Consulate is a lovely little park. The entrance of the Bosphorus University is here too. The grounds used to belong to Robert College, a great high school founded by an American missionary who had baked bread and did the washing for Florence Nightingale's hospital in Üsküdar during the Crimean War.

EMİRGAN

Emirgan is famous for its tulip gardens. Tulips are a symbol of the Ottomans. A white tulip named 'dülbend lale' was taken to Holland by the Ottomans and created a real frenzy there. Dülbend means 'muslin cloth' in Ottoman Turkish. The name tulip comes from this word. This glorious symbol of Istanbul makes the whole city smile every spring. Since the tulip caused the first stock market boom and bust in Holland, it has since been associated with the Dutch as well as the Ottomans.

Just before the second bridge you will notice two castles, one on each side. The one on the European side is Rumelihisarı. Have a look at the Walls of Theodosius chapter for the role they played in the siege of Constantinople.

The beautiful ornate wooden waterfront mansions on the Bosphorus are called 'yalı' from a Greek word meaning seashore. Their boathouses used to be the winter residences of seals breeding around the Princes' Islands and Tuzla.

In 1964, a fisherman, son of a famous wrestler, caught a seven metre long shark nicknamed 'The Monster'. He had a lot of trouble hanging on to his line but didn't give up and eventually two motorboats came to his rescue. 'The Monster' was then displayed at the Galata Bridge.

The name of Jason's legendary ship Argo means 'swift' in Greek. The name of the first Turkish steamboat in the Bosphorus was also 'Swift', after the author of Gulliver's Travels, Jonathon Swift.

The level of the Black Sea is half a metre above that of Sea of Marmara. The Black Sea, fuelled by rivers that empty into it like the Danube, has much lower salt concentration than the Sea of Marmara.

FOOD ALONG THE BOSPHORUS

A real Istanbullu (someone from Istanbul) is someone who knows how to order the right fish at the right time. The bonito, for example, run too deep to be caught in the spring when they are swimming south from the Black Sea. The fishermen get them in autumn on their way back, when they swim closer to the surface and are nice and oily, and that is when you should order them.

The shores of the Bosphorus are still full of fish restaurants serving 'meze', which is a series of small dishes you eat before the main course. They usually arrive on a tray and you can pick and choose whatever takes your fancy.

Börek is a magic word. Flaky, savoury pastries filled with cheese, spinach, beef...you name it. Yeniköy is pastry central! Did I mention the cookies? Do check out Tarihi Yeniköy Börekçisi.

Turkey is famous for its yoghurt (originally a Turkish word), which is available on most boats. Kanlıca on the Asian side is particularly famous. Try it with a heap of sugar on top. Delicious!

Sarıyer is a wonderful place for a stroll and a fish meal. It is towards the entrance of the Black Sea. You can go all the way and have your fish in Rumeli Kavağı on the European side or even Anadolu Kavağı on the Asian side.

PRINCES' ISLANDS

GETTING THERE

No breakfast. None at all! A trip to the islands meant we got one our way when we were kids. It took us ages to get our act together as a family anyway. And there was so much to nibble, munch and crunch that we would skip breakfast and gorge ourselves on the way. There is nothing like a freshly baked simit on the jetty in the morning. A simit is like a bagel covered with sesame seeds. Try to find the vendors which have 'taşfırın' (wood-fired) on their trolleys, the taste is worth seeking out. They also sell 'açma' which is more cakey, softer, more melt-in-the-mouth. Have a cup of tea with one of these and you could easily be mistaken for a local. Then there are the hawkers and peddlers selling anything and everything – lemon squeezers, needle threaders and asparagus peelers - if they can carry it in their pockets, they'll sell it on the ferries. Although they can't match the speed of the hydrofoils, they are much more beautiful and take you back in time to the 19th century when they changed the destiny of these isolated islands forever. Ask your parents to take the ferry instead of the hydrofoil – the trip is really wonderful and you might even see dolphins accompanying the ferry along the way.

During Byzantine and Ottoman times the inhabitants were mainly Greeks, Armenians and Jews. The island came alive with boat races, lavish festivals and parties. The long summers, the pure sea breeze and fresh air, the lack of motor vehicles and the smell of pine trees made this a place of healing and recovery, but that wasn't always the case.

The Byzantines used to call them Papadonisia (priests' islands). This is where they sent royals

who behaved badly for a 'time-out'. Most never saw Constantinople again, some were even blinded before being banished here! Priests, nuns and fishermen who preferred the company of rocks and the sea to that of people lived here too. Constantinople was many hours by dinghy so before the ferries people rarely made the trip. This practice of banishing royalty is one of the stories about how they got the name Princes' islands. Of the 10 islands only 4 are really populated, and one of the others (Sivriada) is a place where stray dogs were banished.

KINALI

The closest island to Istanbul, it was originally called Proti (meaning 'first') by the Byzantines and played host to many naughty emperors and empresses including Romanos Diogenes who couldn't stop Turkish attackers in 1071 and was blinded and banished here. Cycling is a good way to explore the island, and stopping for an ice-cream on the way is a must during summer. It is still popular with Armenians and has the only Armenian Church in the islands.

BURGAZ

The next island along, was named after its ancient watchtower ('pyrgos' in Greek). The Byzantines called it Antigonus after a one-eyed general of Alexander the Great. Women who want to have babies often take the sacred waters from the monastery for help. The beauty of the island inspired many short stories, and there is a legend about a criminal gang and fake banknotes which gave the name to Kalpazankaya (counterfeiter's rocks).

HEYBELİADA

Named after its shape (a saddlebag) this island used to be a retreat for those trying to escape the plague in the 16th century. It also had a treatment centre for TB (tuberculosis) patients. Before antibiotics, what the doctor would order for TB treatment was fresh air and rest. Patients with TB were separated to prevent the spread of the disease and Heybeliada turned out to be the ideal spot. As you approach the island you will see the Turkish Naval Academy and in the main square you may notice the Greek Orthodox Church of St Nicholas, patron saint of mariners, who became popular as Santa Claus.

BÜYÜKADA

The largest island by far, the name literally means 'big island'. It used to be called 'Prinkepos' which can mean both 'prince' and 'principal'. On the two large hills of the island are two major Greek Orthodox monasteries, Hristos (Christ) and Yorgi (St George). The Byzantine Empress Irene of Athens also built a convent on the island and was ironically banished to it years later.

The monastery of St George is so famous that it

has its own day on the 23rd of April, which coincides with one of the major public holidays in Turkey marking the opening of Parliament known and celebrated as Children's Day (Ataturk, the founder of modern Turkey, wanted to entrust the future of the country to the children). Trees along the path to the monastery have thousands of ribbons, strings, hankies and nearly anything else tied to their twigs. You are supposed to leave your worries behind when you tie these decorations on the trees. Legend has it that the priests buried holy relics on the island to keep them safe from invaders. Years later St George is said to have revealed the location of the relics to a shepherd in a dream. The shepherd climbed the hill barefoot and after a bit of a dig around found the relics, including the famous statue of St George killing a dragon. Nowadays it is customary to make a pilgrimage and follow the shepherd's footsteps in silence. Once at the top you can make a wish by taking a candle or a bell. If your wish came true you had to bring your candle or bell back!

It can get pretty crowded here especially on weekends so if possible visit during the week. You can catch a phaeton (horse drawn carriage) from near the jetty and take a tour around the island. Hiring bicycles and walking are also good ways to explore the island, remember cars are not allowed here so it is much safer and more pleasant to ride or walk.

Büyükada reflects the Ottoman spirit of tolerance and has churches, synagogues and a mosque. Did you notice the grand twin domes of the 'Splendid Hotel' on approach? It was used as a hospital during the Crimean War (middle of the 19th century). You can wander through a fairyland of gothic mansions and gingerbread-like houses and homes trying to look like Greek temples showing off their freshly painted colours. Out of some of the houses wafts a language travelling all the way from mediaeval Spain called Ladino, the language of the Turkish Jews. On a balmy spring or autumn afternoon you might hear it coming from bezique (an old card game) tables covered with bulemas and borekas (traditional pastries). You can try some of these pastries yourself at the patisseries on the shopping strip.

In 1929, as tens of thousands of White Russians were escaping Stalin's Red Army, Leon Trotsky (a famous Russian revolutionary) became Büyükada's most famous resident. He was the founder and first commander of the Red Army and played a vital role in the Bolshevik victory in the Russian Civil War of 1918-1920. The tables turned after the war and Trotsky and Stalin became arch enemies. Stalin banished him to Büyükada (seems like everybody has been banished to these islands at some time!) and during his 4 years here he took up fishing and discovered a new species of rockfish and named it after his friend and first premier of the Soviet Union Vladimir Lenin. When he was not busy playing hide-and-seek with Stalin's spies he was busy writing his History of the Russian Revolution.

Another foreign visitor forced to live in Büyükada between 1935 and 1944 helped Jews escape from Nazi occupied Europe. In 1958 he became Pope John XXIII!

INTERESTING MUSEUMS FOR KIDS

There is a lot going on in İstanbul for kids. Google will give you a comprehensive and current list. The following list is for non-Turkish speakers interested in the history of the city.

- **Askeri Müze (Military Museum)** has a fabulous collection including the Byzantine chain to lock off the Golden Horn and cymbals the Mehter (Band of the Sultan's special forces) used. You can listen to the band performances here every afternoon at 3pm. There are artefacts from the First World War, including Gallipolli and a section devoted to Kemal Atatürk, who was an Ottoman general before he embarked on the Turkish War of Independence.
- **Deniz Müzesi (The Naval Museum)** http://www.denizmuzeleri.tsk.tr/ Definitely worth a visit for the magnificient rowboatsof fit for the Sultans.
- **İstanbul Modern** www.istanbulmodern.org/en

Check out the education section on the website to see what's on for kids. They have interesting kids' activities to go with the exhibitions.

- **Mozaik Müzesi (Mosaics of the Great Palace)** http://www.muze.gov.tr/mosaic When the exquisite mosaic floor of the Great Palace of Byzantium was discovered,it made a lot of sense to build a museum over it. The mosaics from the 5th and 6th centuries are full of scenes from daily life. Worth a look to see what kids got up to in Byzantium!
- **Rahmi Koç Müzesi (Rahmi Koç Museum)** www.rmk-museum.org.tr/ This private museum of a keen collector covers anything industrial from all over and inspires and delights at the same time. A retired steam boat serves as a café, there are model train sets, antique toys and if you are into any kind of transport, this place is a must. They also organise weekend boat trips along the Golden Horn in summer.
- **Santral İstanbul Museum of Energy** http://www.santralistanbul.org This is a very happening place. The two engine rooms of an old power plant have been turned into a museum with many interactive displays. It is definitely worth a look.
- **Miniatürk** http://www.miniaturk.com.tr/en/index.php This huge garden has the treasures of Turkey in miniature. It is a nice way to spend an hour or two. There is a little playground and café for a break afterwards.
- **Fetih 1453 (Panorama 1453)** http://www.panoramikmuze.com/en/gallery.php If you have a special

interest in the Ottoman conquest of Constantinople in 1453, check out the website. There are also quite a few videos on Youtube to give you an idea as to what you are in for. It is very engrossing, since it uses music and sound effects for atmosphere.

- **Istanbul Oyuncak Muzesi (Istanbul Toy Museum)** http://www.istanbuloyuncakmuzesi.com/eng/index.html This sweet little museum put together by poet and author Sunay Akın is a great place to remember those far far away times where kids played with toys and one another rather than with iPods and iPads and the rest of it. They offer dolls house workshops, puppet shows, wooden toy painting sessions. Check their website for the list of activities.